Escaping Emily

This is one book from *The Ternion*, a series of novels published in 2024 under the #antiwrimo moniker. Please indulge in the others from the collection:

Spark Bird

Jonathan Koven, Daniel DeRock, Julian Shendelman
ISBN-13: 979-8-9895422-5-3

Julie, or Sylvia

Nicole Tallman, Ibrahim Sofiyullaha, Beryl Cooper
ISBN-13: 979-8-9895422-4-6

Escaping Emily

A Novel

David Estringel
Alexandra Naughton
Risha Mae Ordas

An #antiwrimo Book
Thirty West Publishing House

Escaping Emily

ISBN-13: 979-8-9895422-3-9
Cover art by Jenn Zed
Jacket design by Josh Dale
Edited by Josh Dale
Printed in the U.S.A.

For more titles and inquiries, please visit:
www.thirtywestph.com

Part 1

Written by David Estringel

The room is dark, the air stagnant and thick with lingering traces of lemongrass and lavender from the essential oil diffuser, wedged between a digital alarm clock that glows 11:39 a.m. and a crumple of used tissues on her cluttered nightstand; the musk of two isolated days in bed hangs heavy like a pall. The muted sound of traffic and passers-by reverberate from the curtain-obscured bedroom window facing the street, breaking the silence, rousing her intermittently from the poor-quality sleep that's plagued her since the call. The soft disturbance of footsteps and whispers can be heard outside the bedroom door, sounds Emily Wang had initially found comforting, but now grating the more hours that pass, punctuating the sense of aloneness and void she feels and fears she may never escape. Pulled in by the warmth and womb-like comfort of her ample pillows and oversized down comforter, she struggles to tear herself away and join the land of the living, sitting up in the bed nestling her fatigued body and mind.

Becca, her best friend since childhood, is dead, killed in a car crash on her way back home from a night of partying in Austin, Texas. It was a freak accident. Quick. Random. Becca had been drinking, or the other driver had been, maybe both; it didn't matter. Emily's best friend—for the longest time the better part of her—is gone, and details won't bring her back.

Raising herself to a seated position, after finding the strength, Emily wipes the salty residue of sleep from her eyes, drawn to the stream of light flowing into the room from underneath the bedroom door and the play of shadows that occasionally slice through the glow. The whispers from the other side abruptly come to a halt as three soft raps crack the shell of quiet around her. Then three more. "Emily? Emily?" a concerned voice inquires. "You need to eat something...Emily? It's been two days...Emily?" Like a fog, the voice and shadows dissipate, leaving behind a warm blaze of unmarred illumination that burns her weakened eyes. Shuffling sounds come from the kitchen: the clangs of pans, the clacks of plates, and the *swoops* and *thwacks* of the opening and closing of the refrigerator doors and cabinets.

She leans back with her eyes closed against the upholstered headboard of her queen-sized bed, her hair damp with strands of jet-black adhered to the pale skin of her face. She knows she's been in bed too long, but the solid ground beneath her crumbled to nothing since Becca's mother called on Friday. Emerging from the safety of her sheets seems dangerous somehow; like she had forgotten how to stand, how to breathe. Sleep is her only friend—one that can help her forget—but her dreams betray her, and even during her moments of oblivion all she can think and see is Becca.

"Emily," a familiar voice calls from the hallway, followed by three more discernible knocks on the door. "Emily, I'm going to make lunch. Get yourself together and come out here, so you can eat something. Your father and I are only here for a few more days. We need to talk to you... Lì? We're waiting,"

Emily shakes her head. Annoyed with life, annoyed with death, annoyed with God, and annoyed with that nickname she's always hated.

The world Emily had put on hold held no longer; it's been rummaging through her kitchen in sensible shoes, searching her pantry, refrigerator, and cupboards for something—anything— not 'instant,' microwavable, or smelling of old take-out from The White Lotus, the closest Chinese restaurant that was decent and delivered. It's been sitting in a corner of the apartment with a cup of coffee, hiding behind a newspaper and a stoic veneer. That world is demanding attention, and it's waiting.

"You have no food in this house. Honestly, Lì, how do you live like this?" Mrs. Wang looks at her daughter, thankful for her sudden resurrection but disturbed by the blatant lack of self-care she had fallen into, apparently even before things took such a tragic turn. Shaking her head, she walks over to Emily, cradles her daughter's face in her hands, and insists, "You have to eat."

Emily sits slumped at the kitchen island, having donned an old B-52s t-shirt and gray, fleece sweatpants— her workout clothes—that were on the verge of souring. Her hands in her lap, her left thumb picking at the cuticle of her right one. "We can order in, Māma. Menus are in the utility drawer next to the fridge," Emily instructs as she raises her right arm to point in the general vicinity of the stainless-steel, double-door refrigerator. She can see the frustrated concern on her mother's face as Mrs. Wang takes deliberate steps toward the drawer. "Never mind," she says, her irritation beginning to match that of Mrs. Wang's. "I'll do it."

Stopping mid-step, lifting her hands in surrender, Mrs. Wang acquiesces. "Alright, alright." She pushes past Emily shuffling through the mass of multicolored flyers and menus choking in the utility drawer. She opens the refrigerator door, stands back, and glares at the stark whiteness of the interior. She crinkles her nose at the sparse collection of fragrant, grease-stained cardboard containers interrupting the interior's white, silent scream, subtly shaking her head some more.

"The Chinese around here is pretty good," Emily says, pulling out an oversized, lime green pamphlet with faded, sketchily copied print on its surface.

"Obviously," Mrs. Wang says sarcastically, her stare fixed on a particularly questionable-looking Styrofoam to-go box of half-eaten fried dumplings peeking past two untouched Evian bottles and a blackened, half-eaten banana.

"A meal's not going to magically appear out of thin air, Māma. Not since the last time you checked anyway." Emily closes the utility drawer and lets out a sigh. "Work's been crazy, and I don't have the time to cook much less shop for groceries."

"I'm not saying anything, Lì," Mrs. Wang says, closing

the cold, brushed-metal door. "Your house. Your life."

"Go sit, Māma. This will just take a minute." She gestures over to the lone, mute figure in the living room, the one reading a newspaper atop the chartreuse, mid-century couch anchoring the living room by the sheer power of its vivid color. The faint aroma of black coffee lingers in the air, originating from the Mr. Coffee on the counter near the stove, occasionally letting out a long, drawn-out hiss.

Mrs. Wang tip-toes over to the living room and surveys its contents, as if it were the first time she had laid eyes on anything, then sits at the other end of the couch, clutching a circular, plush, royal blue velvet pillow to her abdomen. "You know," she starts, "I'm not criticizing you, Lì. I just don't understand how you can live like this. I mean, look at this place. Fine furniture. Fancy art on the walls. All this space. But not a single crumb of edible food to be found...anywhere. Of course, we're worried."

Emily enters the living room, pulling her hair back in a crude ponytail, and fastens it with a random elastic band from the utility drawer. Sitting in a matching green chair, she places her hands back in her lap and leans forward. "Look, Māma. I order in at work or grab something on the way home. I don't want to talk about this right now." Emly curls a loose strand of hair behind her right ear. "The food should be here in 45 minutes or so."

"I..."

"Don't," Emily pleaded. "I really can't do this right now. I already explained myself. I do what I need to do to keep all these nice things you're so focused on. You—more than anyone—should be able to understand that."

"Alright alright…You work tomorrow, no? Are you going in?" Mrs. Wang asks, worried about the answer.

"Māma, the funeral. I…"

Mrs. Wang clutches the pillow tighter and lets out a deep, long exhale. "The funeral was this morning, Lì. I spoke to the Chens before your father and I got here. They want to take care of things as quickly as possible. No sense in drawing things out, I suppose. Too painful for too many people."

"What? This morning? How could—"

"You are not doing well, Lì, and the Chens understand that. They know, as well as your father and I do, how close Rebecca and you were, and they know your father and I need to be here for you now. We sent flowers, and we will pay our respects—from you, too—when we get back. No one expects more than that from you right now. They—we—just want you to get through this."

Tears well in Emily's eyes as she looks down at her hands.

"So, you're going in tomorrow?" Mrs. Wang probes.

"Mary," Mr. Wang says, from the other end of the couch, in between page turns of the sport's section.

"I'm just asking a question, John," Mrs. Wang insists. "Just trying to get an idea of what her plan is."

"I suppose I have to. The interview for the promotion I'm going for is tomorrow. I'm supposed to give a presentation, but there's no way I can do it. Not now." Emily wipes the tears from her cheeks, the sting of salt reddening her eyes around the edges.

Mrs. Wang opens her mouth to speak but is interrupted by the disembodied sound of her husband clearing his throat. She looks over at the impenetrable wall of black and white newsprint separating them, and her eyes soften. "No one could fault you for feeling this way, Emily. What happened was—is—awful. Who wouldn't be upset?"

"Thanks, Māma," Emily says, surprised at her mother's uncharacteristic understanding. "I..."

"But, you shouldn't let what happened cripple you like it has. It doesn't do anyone any good. Not for you. Not for your career. Not for..."

"Becca," Emily finishes coldly. Mr. Wang clears his throat again.

"I didn't say that, Lì. You're putting words in my mouth." With a look of discomfort, Mrs. Wang shifts her weight on the cushion beneath her and pulls the pillow in tighter. "All I'm saying is that lying in bed for days and starving yourself won't change anything. You're not going to bring back her life by sacrificing your own." While well-intentioned, Mrs. Wang knows her words crossed a line. Lifting herself from the firm, electric green couch, her black, almost shapeless skirt contrasting against its noise, she moved over to the ottoman in front of Emily's chair and sits. Intuitively, she turns her head to the rustling of paper behind her and asks, "Do you need some water, dear?"

"No, no. I'll wait for the food," Mr. Wang mumbles before falling silent again.

Mrs. Wang takes Emily's right hand—ravaged cuticles and all—and gives it a gentle squeeze. "Rebecca was a lovely girl, and we'll all miss her, especially you. I'm not so far removed from this that I can't understand that, but we need to know that you are going to be ok and not get overwhelmed, get lost...You tend to do that, you know."

"I know," Emily concedes.

"That's why we're here, why we dropped everything when you called. I've never heard you so upset. We felt frightened, Lì. We never want to hear you that way again, God willing."

"It's not any trouble, Lì." Mr. Wang chimes in. "Don't let your mother make things sound worse than they are. We were concerned, that's all. Besides, your brother is there looking after Xiào Lì while we are here. We can stay as long as you like."

"Read your paper, John," Mrs. Wang says.

"Just saying."

Emily pulled her eyes toward her mother and forces a smile.

"It's not for any of us to understand," Mrs. Wang says sternly. "God has a plan for all of us, not for us to question." Mrs. Wang takes Emily's hand again. "Give it to Him. Pray on it. He'll guide you on the right path."

Emily sits erect and stares at her mother with palpable indifference. Her lips curl as if she were about to say something rash, but she quickly recovers. "I know you really believe that, Māma, but I don't think God wants to hear what I have to say to him right now. I'll pass."

As a gasp escapes her mother's lips, the doorbell rings, breaking the awkward quiet of the room. The bell rings again, followed by a muffled "Uber Eats for Emily Wang?"

Emily looks at her mother's shocked face, then the quiet fortress of solitude of her father and gets up to answer the door. "Let me get your water, Bàba."

***

The atmosphere at Harker and Associates, Los Angeles' premier advertising agency, is always electric around the holidays, especially Christmas. While the décor generally never diverged from the ultra-modern vibe that the agency had become so famous for in their work and approach to marketing—metallic trees, silver garlands, and abstract ornaments—sparse hints of the staff's tastes and actual priorities manage to sprout up among the cubicles and desks throughout the agency like clusters of mistletoe on errant treetops. Across the board, deadlines loom, and projects wrap up to facilitate visits home, staycations, and long-planned ski trips to Vale and Taos. Most everyone who doesn't dwell in the upper echelons of management is eager to put last-minute touches on their work before taking long-deserved rests—thanks to the company's generosity and annual proclivities toward merry-making– save one.

Emily stands within her spartan cubicle, its only decoration a wrapped candy cane in her pencil cup and a large, white plastic cup emblazoned with "Ho! Ho! Ho!" in big red letters, a remnant from the office Christmas party the day before. With intensity and focus, she gathers belongings from her desktop and hanging cabinets and meticulously places them in cardboard boxes she fetched from the mailroom earlier that day. She grabs a small picture frame propped next to her computer screen, blowing invisible dust from the glass's surface. She fingers the smooth, cream-colored ceramic frame that contained a picture of her parents, brother, and her, taken on the day of her graduation from USC. She remembers the bittersweetness of the day: the excitement of walking on the stage, the disappointment of Becca not being beside her. "Huh? What was that?" she blurts, pulled from her brief reverie.

"I asked if your packing was going all right?'" a well-groomed, middle-aged man with thinning hair and graying temples repeats. "Exciting news, your promotion, no?

"Oh, yes. Definitely, Shaun. I didn't think I would get it. I mean, I hoped, but it was a surprise to say the least." Emily places the frame face down on her desk.

"I should hardly think so," Shaun chuckles. "You earned it, I must say. You manage your accounts smoothly and potential, high-dollar clients ask for you by name. Hell, even some of mine have asked about you. Don't get any funny ideas though. Ha! I know where you work. But, really, you make your people happy, and that makes 'the powers that be' happy. Simple math, my friend. You are on your way to being one of them, I must say." Shaun looks at Emily's forlorn expression, rounding the cubicle's corner and leaning against the partition wall. "You ok? Not nervous, are you? Naw, you'll do fine."

"I'm fine, Shaun," Emily recovers, sensing what she must have looked like. "It's just a lot, you know? New job, moving offices...holidays. Blah, blah, blah." She feigns a chuckle.

"Yeah, yeah, I get it...and?" Shaun had only known Emily for less than a year but long enough to identify such a significant shift in mood. Even as a newbie at the agency, she had always approached her engagement with peers—and her work—with a focus and at least a surface joviality that put others at ease. Now, there was a void—a distance—that replaced the hum she typically brought into a room. "I don't want to sound all trippy and New Agey and stuff, but your energy is off. Way off, I must say. Different. You know? Something goin' on?"

Emily rests her left hand on the overturned frame, tapping it rhythmically with her index finger. "Yeah, maybe a bit. Not really looking forward to going back home to Aliso Viejo. Holidays and family blah blah blah. Not very original. I don't know. The whole thing can be exhausting...stressful...with my family anyway. Here," she says, offering the cold, ceramic encasement to Shaun. "I'm supposed to leave tonight."

"Yeah, family bullshit never gets easier, does it? It's as much a custom of the season as eggnog and credit card debt, I'm afraid. They know you too well, and you them, but those are the cards we're dealt. Just gotta make the best of it, Emily, and remember they're the ones that have your back in the end, even if they are massive pains in the ass. At least that's the idea that gets me through the holidays every year relatively sober." Shaun flips the frame and looks at the picture. "Handsome family. Look very proud of you. Why, they don't look so bad."

Emily chuckles. "No, they don't, do they?" She reaches out and takes the picture back, sliding it into the box somewhere between her red leather organizer and a borrowed copy of *Crucial Conversations* that she forgot to return to a recently fired coworker, Jarvis Linney, who occupied a cubicle across the room near the employee lounge. "And you? Any plans for Christmas?"

Shaun looks at his watch and frowns. "The wife's picking me up. Supposed to have been here twenty minutes ago, but you know how it goes. Holiday traffic. Last-minute shopping. It could be hours before she gets here. Regardless, we're staying put. Doing the whole 'tree thing' and having friends and family come over. You're welcome to stop by if you decide to nix your plans. Better than being alone." The look on Shaun's face is sympathetic and slightly embarrassed about the familial can of worms he kicked over. In an attempt to redirect the conversation, he transitions to safer subject matter. "Hey, Emily, you excited?"

"About?"

"Your new position, silly. Director of Marketing. And moving into that sweet, new office of yours. Plenty of green-eyed monsters roaming the halls because of that, I must say. Well? You excited?"

"It'll be a challenge—that's for sure—but I can handle it."

"Yes, you can. Don't sweat it. They chose the right person for the job. Just don't forget us 'little guys' here on the frontlines." Shaun grins and gives Emily a cordial punch on her left shoulder, unconsciously attempting to distract her from the glints of green in his smiling brown eyes.

"You got it, Shaun. Thanks."

"No problem. Seriously, though, I am happy for you."

"I know."

"And the invite still stands. Plenty of room at the Murphy house this Christmas. No reason to be alone this time of year if you can avoid it. Not on Christmas anyways." Clumsily, he pulls his phone from his back pocket and scrolls through his messages. "Ah, and she buzzes. The wife's downstairs. Like I said, last-minute shopping. Those kids of ours are gonna make out like bandits this year, I must say." Shaun slips his phone back into the back pocket of his trousers and begins to walk away. "See you next year, Madame Director. Tell your family Merry Christmas for me...if you go that is." He rounds the corner near the elevators and disappears into the dimly lit lobby with a *ping.*

Emily stares at the corner lost in thought, her attention turned toward the darkened, glass-walled office across from the twin doors Shaun vanished through. Her new office is waiting. She returns to her packed box, pulls the framed picture back out, and gives it another look. *Why they don't look so bad,* echoed in her head, as she haphazardly dropped the frame into the box. *No, they don't, do they?*

Walking toward the elevators, Emily fixes her eyes on the blackness of her new office's interior. She approaches the glass wall and looks inside, her right hand shielding her eyes from the glare of fluorescent lights overhead. Empty except for the newly dusted, vogueish furniture that came with all administrative offices in the agency: cold, sleek, and devoid of personality. She tries to picture herself sitting behind the metal and glass desk and how she might decorate it and the walls, but she can't. Her mind—like her office—is empty, devoid of warmth and personality.

She presses the down button, but the elevator takes its time to get to her. Emily cocks her head upward and waits for the plastic down-arrow above the doors to glow green, for the *ping* to bring the day to an end. Tapping her right index finger on the strap of her purse, she recounts her encounter with Shaun and snickers, finding his holiday outlook on life to be well-intentioned but too saccharine to swallow. *Ping.* The elevator doors opened. Emily enters and turns around to face the void outside herself waiting for her return after the holiday. As the doors close, she reaches over to the button panel to her right and presses "P1." *Doesn't he know you can be alone anywhere?* she thinks to herself, looking straight ahead as the new darkness in her life shrinks away with another *ping.*

***

Standing in the doorway, wrapped in the snug warmth of a form-fitting, wool peacoat and caramel-colored Coach suitcases in each hand, Emily lets her eyes adjust to the surrounding murk, while the room's smell unlocks doors in her mind to her childhood. In unison, her bags drop to the freshly vacuumed, taupe-colored carpet, followed by an anxious drawn-out sigh. Instinctively, she extends her right hand beyond the borders of the door frame, and with an expert flick of a finger, there is light.

Her bedroom has not changed an iota since she had last seen it about five years ago, except for two medium-sized cardboard boxes stacked in the far-right corner between a 5-shelf, custom-made bookcase painted white and a window with its blind pulled down. Same bed, same ornate headboard, same simple, pale pink bedspread. Certificates and academic awards from high school pepper the walls like buckshot. Emily walks over to the bookcase, places her still-gloved hand on top, and gives it a slight shake, impressed that it still maintains the sturdiness she remembers. Finger by finger, she pulls off her gloves—first right, then left—and runs the index finger of her right hand across the exposed spines of her old, familiar "friends," speed-reading titles and authors. She slides her fingers across *Great Expectations* and *Jude the Obscure*, stopping at *Where Angels Fear to Tread* to rub away a smudge with some friction and bit of spit, then taps the spines of *Metamorphosis* by Ovid, and *Slaughterhouse Five*. A slight smile curves the sides of her mouth as the stale smell of aged wood and enamel paint tickles her nostrils. Squatting down, she surveys the content of the shelf below. With greater care, she scans the lettering from left to right, stopping midway at a relatively thin, worn-edged paperback. The curves of her mouth extended as she pulled the book from the shelf, sensing hints of dust that managed to escape her mother's most diligent efforts around her eyes and nose. Turning her wrist, she reverently read its title, *Where I'm Calling You From*.

Emily unbuttons her coat and sits on the edge of the bed. The metallic groans of aged springs pull her further into a dubiously happier time. Her smile slowly begins to fade as a heaviness settles upon her brow. With the book on her lap, she slides her right index finger underneath the softened front cover up and down the cardstock back. Her thumb brushes the smudged, top curled-up corner as she bites her slightly chapped lower lip. Sliding her finger further in under the cover, she flips it to the left to expose a title page with something written across it, diagonally, like an author's signature:

Make sure you give this back, bitch!
Love,
B

A tremble of emotion takes over Emily's body. Her lips expel an amalgamation of choked-back laughter, tears, and repressed grief, aided by the two vodka tonics she downed at the bar before arriving at her childhood home. Emily's eyes sting as her vision begins to blur, the back of her right hand instinctively brushes away the moisture before it could stain her pale cheeks. She remembers how Rebecca raved about the book for days after she read it during their senior year, going on and on about its depth and realism. Never being one for short stories, Emily passed on giving it a read. Rebecca, however, was persistent and swore that reading Raymond Carver would change Emily's life. She was right. Carver quickly became a regular occupant of Emily's backpack for the rest of the school year. Moreover, it became a regular escape when life became too much, and she needed an escape.

Emily deliberately thumbs through story titles anchoring her in the familiarity of lighter times: "Nobody Said Anything." "Little Things." "What We Talk About When We Talk About Love." Flashes streak across her mind bringing an authentic smile and a flutter to her chest: pineapple gummi bears, mattress contraband—mostly junk food and a pack of Marlboro Lights that took the two a little over a year to smoke—and talking on the phone all night until someone fell asleep. For the first time—in a long time—the feeling of 'home' doesn't seem like a cruel echo sounding from the absence she's been carrying with her. A melancholy begins to come over her as she realizes the warmth of waxing nostalgia won't last, and the room's chill sets in.

"Emily, get your skinny ass down here!" a deep voice bellows from downstairs, pulling her out of her head. "Or, are you smoking out the window for ol' time's sake?"

"Ugh!," Emily huffs, as she slams the paperback shut. "Such a pain, Michael!"

***

The afternoon sky is pale gray with fingers of cloud that stretch across its expanse like wispy pulls of rolled cotton. Bay trees flank the front porch and cast a palpable shadow across its surface, cloaking the forest-green porch swing, and a pensive figure in an icy dimness that isolates them from the surrounding world. Emily sits at the far-right corner of the swing, using the tip of her right boot to rock herself, rhythmically, to the sound of distant traffic and the winter breeze through bare, lichen-kissed branches. The screen door, also green, swings open, and a broad back emerges with steaming mugs of coffee suspended in the air by curled fingers of each hand. "Shocker! This has never really been an almond milk kind of house, so I had to cut the bitterness with something else," the deep voice consoles.

"Non-dairy creamer?"

"Geez, Em, no," her brother Michael says and turns to face her with an exaggerated expression of disgust on his face. "You have been away too long." He hands her a cup and sits at the other end of the swing, watching her take a sip.

"Mmm," Emily almost purrs, her tense body softly melting as if surrendering to a long-needed hug. "Bailey's. You're right, I forgot." A smile threatens to appear on her face but doesn't. She had forgotten about the legendary bottle of Bailey's Original Irish Cream that mysteriously appears in the Wang refrigerator every December—the only time a drop of alcohol could ever be found under the Wang roof. She's always amused by how the bottle seemed to replenish itself without anyone taking the credit. The phenomenon has been a long-standing part of Wang family mythology that included nocturnal deposits by the tooth fairy, an almost religious reverence for the number 7, and Mrs. Wang's systematic descent into madness by a decades-long battle with *duwendes*, or house gremlins, whose main objective was to hide her car keys at the most inconvenient times.

"Settling in ok?" Michael asks after an uncomfortable pause. He takes a long sip and fixes his gaze on the old bay across the porch. "I'm supposed to tell you that the sheets are fresh, and you can find more—plus clean towels—in the upstairs linen closet. Sorry if the room's a bit musty; I was supposed to air it out earlier, but I got caught up with errands after I dropped off Māma and Bàba at Xiào Lì this morning. I was also supposed to do something else...but...yeah, completely out of my head. It'll come to me, eventually." Michael takes another long sip and leans forward trying to catch Emily's eye. "It ok? The coffee?"

Mid-gulp, Emily places her right hand on her chest, fingers splayed out, "Just the thing," she says. "It's really good." She rests the mug on her lap and cradles it with her gloved hands. She turns to face him; a warmth spreading across her center. "I should ask you the same. You haven't been back from the Philippines long. How was school?" She drinks in the details of Michael's face, many of which mirrored her own, especially his amber-colored eyes that showed greener when exposed to the cold or tears.

"Aw, it was alright. Not a big deal. Tough. You know. The professors were pretty awesome. Learned a ton. The people, however, were amazing. I think I learned more from them to be honest."

Emily looks down at the cooling contents of her mug, strands of black hair slipping past her left ear.

"I interned at one of the largest public health clinics in Manila doing immunization outreach and community mobilization during my last two semesters there. Really fucking amazing." Michael eagerly searches her face for something not there then pulls his eyes away to look toward the screen door, taking a last sip.

"Yeah?"

"Yeah...So, how is it, being back home, now? You know, after Becca and everything."

Emily looks to her right past the lawn of dying grass and patches of brittle brown leaves toward the street. "I really don't want to talk about that, Mike."

"Cool. Cool," he backtracks, "Hey, I did some really cool things, while I was away. Still want to do more...when I get the chance."

"So, you're going back then? Sounds like that's the plan, like you want to."

Michael looks down into his empty cup and licks his lips. "Sure, at some point."

"Right," Emily responds, shifting her weight and angling her body more toward him. "Māma says you're taking classes now for a Doctorate of Clinical Psychology. That's great, Mike. We can use all the help we can get." She gives his right knee light taps with the knuckles of her left hand. "Way to show me up, little brother. Really. That's amazing. So, you'll go back afterward, then?"

Her brother turns to look at her and smiles but doesn't look directly into her eyes. "Grad school is going to take a while, and I'm pretty fried with school. Kinda need a break. You know? So, all that's 'on hold' for a minute. Besides, the folks need help with the store and stuff, and I'm here."

"Mike..."

"Nah, It's alright. It's not a bad deal, really: I help out for a few days during the week and on weekends, and I take classes online at night. The pay sucks—you know how cheap

Bàba is—but they're covering the cost of school, and I don't have to worry about room and board. A lot of people would kill for a gig that sweet. Besides, I can do more going back to the Philippines as a therapist. Just have to bide my time."

"True that, Emily says. "Wait, why do they need your help? Things okay with them? The store?"

"They're just getting older, that's all," Michael says. "Bound to happen sooner or later. I'm trying to talk the old man into hiring someone else—at least part-time—but you know how that goes."

"Sounds about right."

"Anyway, I hear you're kicking ass at work, according to Māma at least. Director of Marketing. Not bad, Em. You excited?"

The familiar question makes Emily keenly aware of the cold air on her face and the rising heat beneath her wool coat. She looks down again into her half-filled cup and shrugs. "Sure, it's what I've been working toward. Everything's going according to plan, so what's not to be excited about? I told Māma not to make a big deal about it."

Michael nods and laughs. "So, of course, she activated the church lady phone tree after you hung up."

Emily gives her brother's knee a good thwack with the back of her left hand.

"Oh, don't be cross. She's proud of you; that's all. Besides, you know how things work: A win for you is a win for the family."

"A win for us," Emily says. "A PsyD is a pretty big deal,

little brother."

"Yeah, well, it's harder to convince folks that your child is poised to conquer the world when he's standing behind a register and stocking shelves on the regular."

"C'mon, Mike. Don't do that. This isn't a race. Anyway, there isn't much you could do to convince them you didn't hang the moon. I still can't believe how you managed to get them to send you so far away to school. If they would've had their way, I would have been stuck living at home and gone to some community college near here."

Michael laughed. "Well, they obviously recognized my remarkable maturity and intellect."

"Yeah, I don't know. I'm pretty sure your penis had something to do with it."

Pretending to gasp, Michael gives Emily's left knee a thwack with the knuckles of his right hand. "Bitch!"

Emily chuckles.

"Still, you ended up doing well for yourself. Really well, in fact. You went to Los Angeles and never looked back."

"Only because I applied to the university behind their backs and got all that lovely scholarship money. Otherwise, I never would have been able to leave. You know that."

The cold air suddenly became tinged with a bitter chill, a silence growing between the two.

Emily pulls the errant strands of hair back behind her ear. "Still paying for that one."

Michael leaned back and crossed his legs. "Well, you do have quite the knack for making power moves."

Emily turns her face and stares into her brother's eyes. "Like going to the Philippines to school?"

Michael laughs nervously. "Not the same."

"Only because they agreed to send you without a second thought. Some of us had to throw down a gauntlet."

"They still giving you shit about that then?"

"The passive aggression gets doled out in dribs and drabs, but Māma manages to get her jabs in now and then."

"Yeah, that tracks." Michael leans forward, eyes fixed on the old bay tree, empty cup cradled in his hands. "That's just her way. Maybe try not to be so sensitive?"

Emily scoffs. "Toxic masculinity really is an ugly color on you, not to mention so 2020."

"And success makes your ass look fat," her brother chuckles. "Anyway, hopefully, both of us can get back to where we want to be sooner than later. Things aren't all that bad, I guess. I'm just restless. Impatient...maybe a little sad,"

"Well, it sounds to me like you're going for something you really love. Really—sibling rivalry aside—I think that's amazing. Not everyone does that. Not everyone is that brave. Trust me on that one." With slight hesitation, she takes her brother's hand and catches his gaze. "I know I haven't been around a whole lot—with work and all—but from what I know, Māma and Bàba are really proud of you, and so am I."

"Yeah?"

"Yeah," Emily cajoles, "which is unbelievable on so

many levels given your tendencies toward being a slacker and inconsistent follow-through."

"Still such a bitch!" he exclaims with his mouth agape and a bit of a giggle.

"What?" Emily teases. "It's true. You got both your ears pierced in high school, and those sad, little studs didn't last a day before you took them out."

"Bàba grounded me until I have grandchildren."

"Oh, my God! And that backstreet, flying dragon tattoo down the spine of your back you got in Jakarta? How you walked away from that without a case of hepatitis, I'll never know. By the way, don't ever send me pictures that gross again."

Michael laughs. "I'm surprised Māma didn't make sure I would ever have grandchildren, thank you."

"Have either of them ever seen it? Do you even own a tank top?" she continued to poke.

"Not in this house," Michael insists, putting his arm around his sister for the first time in a long time—both a little drunk from laughter and the holiday magic of their spiked coffees. "I'm really glad you're here, Em. I've missed you. We all have."

"Same," Emily admits as she lies her head on Michael's shoulder, cognizant—for the first time in a long time—of what 'home' used to feel like.

***

Christmas dinner at the Wang house—at least from what Emily can remember—is a meticulously orchestrated, lackluster event that plays itself out every 24th of December like a residual haunting. Mrs. Wang wakes up before anyone else in the house—4 a.m. to be exact—to commence preparations for the day. She goes downstairs to the kitchen to make herself some tea and refresh Bao's (the family's, seven-year-old ragdoll cat that looked more like a cream puff) food and water dishes. Then prepares herself a small breakfast of buttered toast with raspberry preserves and black coffee, and follows it with a round of light, yet thorough, cleaning of the home's first floor—a supplemental maneuver carried over from the deep-cleaning the night before that ensures no rogue crumbs or settled dust particles can take root and multiply before the string of holiday well-wishers and dinner guests find their way onto the Wang's doorstep.

Food prep and cooking starts after everyone wakes up; a process facilitated by Mrs. Wang's vacuuming of the house's second story. Wrap-up generally occurs sometime around 6 p.m. when everyone finds themselves back upstairs to get ready for the night's festivities: dinner and midnight mass.

The usual suspects always attend: the Niedermeyer's, a kind older couple who had lived next door since California was a state and who were gracious enough to help the family get settled when they relocated to Orange County from a small, rural town in Texas; Albert Schwartz, a 54-year-old professional bachelor and non-practicing Jew, who was also the Wang's bookkeeper since Xiào Lì opened. Sadly, he had no one to spend the holidays with except his six temperamental—and very spoiled—dachshunds; The Chens; Rebecca's parents; and Bao, who was well aware that his invitation was inferred. All were welcome and considered to be no less than family.

Traditionally, Mr. Wang is usually nowhere to be found that day, even though he always closed Xiào Lì at noon. More of an obstacle to his wife's annual routine, he finds it best to keep out of the way and emerge, as if out of thin air, just minutes before the dinner guests arrive. In the past, he would hit a double feature on his way home from work or linger and rearrange inventory in Xiào Lì's stockroom—anything but get caught up in the kinetic energy that emanated from the kitchen into every room of the house.

The past couple of years, however, his disappearances limited themselves to the boundaries of home, especially the double-car garage that regularly housed the family cars, Michael's and his, along with motley family treasures that were useless in function but priceless in sentimental value. Except for Xiào Lì being closed that Christmas Eve, this year is no different. Mr. Wang makes his way to his sanctum sanctorum shortly after Mrs. Wang's Hoover starts roaring in the hallway just outside of Michael's room, the first expanse of carpet up for grabs from the top of the staircase. He perches himself on a simple, wooden chair at the wall opposite the automatic door, where a long, narrow, wooden table extends itself along its width, topped with a variety of dusty gardening tools; bags of potting soil; tightly capped mason jars full of old nails, screws, doohickies, and thingamabobs; and an old pair of gloves that had seen better days. He loves gardening and often looks at his tools as almost extensions of his own hands.

Notes of classical music hang thickly in the air like evening stars, softly streaming from the cracked window of Mr. Wang's 1980s cream-colored Ford LTD that he swears still worked like new but doesn't. One by one, he picks up the implements—first a spade, second a pair of pruning shears—and dusts them with a rag he keeps in a bagful on the hanging shelf above. He can hear the clanking of pans and closing of cabinets through the closed door leading to the kitchen, and the creaks of footsteps, differing in cadences and weight from the ceiling above. The sounds fill him with warmth. Words are being exchanged—directives, excuses, and apologies—but where (or who) they came from he can't tell. Quizzically, he turns toward his work table to grab a neglected hand rake and notices caked mud on the stiffened cloth in his left hand. He holds it under his nose and sniffs, overcome by the strong smell of mildew; it had been used before, some time ago. When? He couldn't tell.

***

The Wang's kitchen becomes unbearably warm sometime around noon. All the stove's burners are lit and hard at work simmering, boiling, and sautéing the various contents of cast-aside Tupperware bowls congregating, in desperate need of a wash, around the sink. The transformation of a 20-pound, self-basting turkey is well underway within the spotless confines of the oven and filling the stifling air of the cozy room with a savory optimism making every moment of discomfort worthwhile. The window above the sink is opaque with condensation, further obscured by steam rising from a strainer full of quartered boiled potatoes cooling just underneath in the sink. Abstract shapes and shifts of light and shadow draw the eye and hint at another world happening on the other side of the glass.

"You're cutting those too big," Mrs. Wang says as she briefly turns her face from the stovetop—spoon in hand—to spy Emily's less-than-agile attempt at dicing onions for her well-reputed sage and pork sausage stuffing.

Emily, wearing a navy, cable-knit sweater, vintage-style jeans, and sweat socks, is at the kitchen table, intently rolling a kitchen knife up and down in rhythmic chops. "They're fine, Māma. I can give them another once-over after I am done, if you like." Though annoyed, Emily maintains a laser focus on the task before her, hyperconscious of the plastic bowl of onion wedges waiting next to her mother's wooden cutting board.

Mrs. Wang turns again, her upper body following with

a twist at the waist. Her eyes survey the contents of the bowl and the fragmented heap spilling over the board's sides. She turns and commences lifting pot lids and sprinkling in herbs that she had pulled—one by one like flowers—from the spice cabinet above. "They look big to me. Stuffing shouldn't be crunchy. The bigger the pieces, the longer they take to cook. Crunchy. You want crunchy stuffing?"

Exasperated, Emily drops the knife onto the cutting board without flourish and pushes the tear-inducing slab of wood away from her as if it were a ravaged dinner plate. Blowing away a strand of jet hair that fell before her eyes, she gets up and heads toward the window, captivated by the blurry scene behind its hazy glow. "I need to give my hands a break before I do the rest. Want some coffee?" she asks, pulling two mugs from the dish rack. She extends her right palm to the sweaty glass and brushes it back and forth, exposing the distorted form of Michael raking leaves in the backyard."

"Lì, I just cleaned that this morning, and now it will be all smudged. Honestly!"

"I'll clean it in a sec, Māma," Emily assures. "That's weird. Why is Mike raking the backyard? That's Bàba's thing. He won't like that." She is overcome by the urge to find the bottle of glass cleaner tucked away somewhere under the sink but suppresses it.

"I asked your brother to do it. Your father had a very busy day yesterday and needs his rest. I swear that man will drive himself into the ground if he has his way, but what do

I know? I am making him take it easy today. He'll show his face sooner or later."

"Where is he?"

"How should I know? I need him to rest, not cook." Mrs. Wang decisively pulls two pots from the stovetop and replaces them with new ones to boil water for iced tea.

Emily resumes her surveillance of Michael. She gives the widow three rapid knocks, grabbing his attention. *What are you doing?* she mouths from her side of the world. Her brother smirks as he looks over his sister's shoulder and catches an icy stare from his mother. The grin remains, but his eyes convey a blend of discomfort and awkwardness, which Emly immediately understands. Once Mrs. Wang looks away and returns to her monitoring of the evening's side dishes, Michael rests the rake on his right shoulder, pulls off his glove with his teeth, and flips Emily the middle finger. Grinning harder, he pulls his glove over his hand and resumes.

Such a dork, Emily says to herself, then catches herself grinning just as goofily. She hadn't noticed before, but the yard, like the front lawn, was strangely out of sorts: the trees in need of pruning, and it seems like neither side of the house had seen a rake in months. "Bàba should try to relax more and not work so hard. Both of you should. The yards must be driving him crazy. There has to be someone around here that does lawn work."

Mrs. Wang lets out a contained, "Multiple, probably."

"Mike said he's been trying to get you guys to hire

someone part-time for the store. It's not a bad idea, Māma. You should…"

"No need," Mrs. Wang interrupts, opening the oven door to check on the turkey. "Your brother is here and helps when he can. Thank God he has the sense to stay close to his family." Mrs. Wang turns to face Emily, pouring coffee and shaking her head. "Besides, the holidays are almost over, so things at Xiào Lì will die down soon enough…Speaking about work, are you ready to start your new job?"

"I've been there for almost five years already, Māma. It's not a big deal," Emily insists. "Same agency. Same people. Different office." She walks over to the counter near the refrigerator and leans against it, taking a long sip. "Everything is going according to plan. It'll be fine."

"Oh," Mrs. Wang retracts.

"What?"

"Nothing."

"No, Māma," Emily says as she places her coffee mug down on the counter. "That was a loaded 'oh.' Go ahead and say it."

Mrs. Want uncovers a red Dutch oven on one of the backburners and briskly stirs its contents. "I don't have anything to say about anything…although I do wonder why I seem more excited about your success than you do." Mrs. Wang's stirs turn more into stabs that finally stop once Emily lets out a frustrated sigh.

"Here we go," Emily says under her breath.

"Here we go, nothing. I can't talk about what I see? You aren't making it difficult, but you get upset when I notice. You walk around like a captive in your own home and get offended anytime I ask you about your life. I suppose I should just stop talking altogether."

Emily throws her hands up in the air. "God, you are being so dramatic right now!"

Mrs. Wang stares at her daughter, as if into a mirror, and raises her eyebrows.

Emily averted her eyes to keep from glaring. She walks back to the window with the hope of anchoring herself to her brother's image, but he's gone. "I'm sorry, Māma. I shouldn't be cross." Still not looking in her mother's direction, she grabs her now lukewarm mug and clutches it to her abdomen. "You're right: I'm not as excited as I should be about the promotion, and I could have less of an attitude. Just overwhelmed, I guess. Too much change too soon."

Mrs. Wang's eyes soften, and her grip on the spoon loosens. "I know, Lì. What's happened to bring all this on?"

"I don't know...I'm just not happy in general, I guess. Haven't been for a while."

"Oh..."

"Jesus, Māma!"

"What, daughter? You tell me you're unhappy, and I am not supposed to react?" Mrs. Wang chastises. "How convenient for you."

"Well, I am not happy, Māma, and there is nothing convenient about it."

"What do you have to be unhappy about, Lì? You have a good job, a beautiful home, lovely things. You don't need anyone, and you come and go…as you please. God should smile upon all of us like that for all the appreciation you show. He's been very good to you, given you everything you wanted, everything you asked for." Mrs. Wang crosses her arms and exhales deeply.

"How can you look me in the face and ask me that? Your memory can't be that bad."

Mrs. Wang remains stoic though she can't help but avoid Emily's stare.

"Well, maybe LA doesn't make me happy anymore," Emily claimed.

"Then move back home if you are so miserable," Mrs. Wang offers. "If that's really how you feel."

"Right," Emily mocks. "I moved to LA to get away from this place. The last thing I need to do is crawl back here with my tail between my legs." She regrets the words the second they left her lips.

"And look at you now. Lots of people would give anything to have the life you have, and they'd be more grateful for it. Honestly, Emily." Mrs. Wang unfolds her arms to return to her stovetop.

"Like Michael." The words leave Emily's mouth before she can stop them.

Mrs. Wang faces her daughter, eye-to-eye, and delivers a stare pinning her daughter's feet to the ground. "Yes, exactly like your brother." Mrs. Wang calmly reaches behind her back, unties her apron, and tosses it over one of the kitchen table chairs. "I think you've done enough for one day," she declares. "People will start arriving in a few hours. I'm going to go lie down."

"Māma, c'mon," Emily starts as she grabs the knife from the cutting board. "I'll just finish…"

"No," Mrs. Wang says exiting the kitchen toward the staircase. "I'll fix them when I come back down."

A chill takes over the kitchen as Emily stands there alone with the muffled sounds of clattering and sputtering from simmering pots. Her eyes pull to the shrinking refrigerator, sole witness to the flaying that just occurred, and she considers the magical bottle awaiting her inside and the spell it could cast upon her—if at least momentarily. She wants to cry, unsure if the feeling stems more from the guilt she felt or the onion autopsy on the cutting board.

***

Emily lies on her side on top of her blush bedspread, properly buzzed from multiple swigs of Bailey's Irish Cream, and watches the shadows of leaves from the old cottonwood outside dance upon the window screen. She is exhausted, depleted of all energy and motivation to finish out the day with people from her past—and present—who seem like relative strangers to her save Michael. Everything she feared, everything that filled her with such dread and anxiety, was realized during the sparring match with her mother—a repeat performance of an old tune dating back as far as she can remember. Her eyes tear up as *I'm not happy* re-plays in her head; it was a truth she had never voiced to anyone before, much less herself. The sheer gravity of the words crushes her into the mattress like a bug under God's thumb, her limbs leaden. She hears shuffling outside the closed door of her bedroom as if someone were lingering. Emily raises her head and turns her gaze toward the crack under the door, where light from the hallway sieves its way through tangles of taupe-colored shag. She sees the movement of something—someone—but before she can sit up, all is still; the bar of light between the floor and door glows brighter, unobscured.

As she gets out of bed, she uses her hands to brace herself and digs her fingers into the hard edge of the mattress. With a sudden rush of blood from her head to her feet, the periphery of the already dim room grows darker, promising to close in on her. A ringing fills her ears, as a slight spinning forces her to sit down and center herself for a moment. A bright haze takes over her vision, intensifying until the room's darkness bleeds into it and restores balance. Counterintuitively, Emily grabs the opened bottle from the fridge that she had tucked between the bed and the nightstand and takes another swig. The thick liquid is warm on her tongue but hot going down. She winces, remembering how awful the stuff tastes when room temperature—the paradox of the brown bottle: liquid gold ice cold, solvent stain remover when it's not.

Emily gives herself a bounce and launches herself from the mattress into a standing position. She glances at the digital clock on the nightstand, which reads 6:27 p.m., and heads over to the closet, pulling the elastic band from her ponytail and running her fingers through her hair. The clangs and bangs of metal pots and tops sound from the kitchen below, reminding her that there is unfinished business to take care of.

Emily slides open the mirrored door of her closet and rakes hanger after hanger to the left across the metal bar across its width, inspecting each piece quickly but thoroughly. "Black, something black," she mutters, finally settling on a simple but elegant Nordstrom dress she had years before for a company function. Tasteful yet flattering to the figure, refined yet contemporary. Very Emily.

She closes the closet door, brings the hanger up beneath her chin, and slightly leaning backward lets the dress mold itself to her body. Carefully inspecting her reflection, content with her choice, she walks toward her suitcase on the floor at the foot of her bed and digs out a black cashmere shrug and a pair of fine black flats. Pleased, she tosses the outfit on the bed and makes her way around to the nightstand for another swig of courage before changing. As she catches her reflection in the vanity mirror across from her, she notices how different it seems, but can't put her finger on what changed. Tidier, perhaps, except for her red leather makeup bag and the sprawl of makeup that had made its way across its surface. Emily takes another sip and places the bottle back down.

Making her way across the room, the mirror appears larger, capturing more of the room than usual. She sits down, her eyes fixed on the mirror's frame, and follows the white-enameled curvature of it. "No," she says quietly. "Where are they?" She opens each vanity drawer and rummages through its contents, shuffling around pens, old movie tickets, elastic bands, and petrified jelly beans with her frantic fingers. "Where are they," she asks the air, her voice growing in volume. She darts from her chair to her old dresser and looks through its drawers with the same intensity and determination, slamming each one shut with every fruitless attempt. Emily's eyes desperately scan the room for possibilities but find none. Frustrated and confused, she makes her way back to vanity and sits down in disbelief. She looks at herself with her furrowed brow and teary eyes, as if the image behind the glass has an answer, when in a corner of the reflection, she sees them, the two cardboard boxes.

Both cardboard containers were securely taped, requiring Emily to dig the car keys out of her purse to cut through the center seams of the box tops. Impatiently, she runs her house key down the top of the larger one and rips the flaps open. One after the other, Emily pulls items out and tosses them over her shoulder: old sweaters, jeans, even a couple of purses...but no pictures. Looking at the side of the box, she realizes, according to the Magic Marker print on one of its sides, that it and its contents were destined for the Salvation Army. *They have to be in the small one*, she assured herself internally. Attacking the small container with the same fervor as the first, she hears things—denser things—sliding about, clacking against the box's stiff interior walls. After tearing through the tape, a jumble of loose photos, greeting cards, and various plastic trinkets from amusement parks, gumball machines, and school dances are revealed—all mementos from her youth, better times, of Rebecca and her together.

"Fuck." A deep voice says under breath from over Emily's shoulder. Michael stands in the open doorway with a regretful expression on his face. "I was supposed to take those down to the garage before you got here. Damn it, Em. I'm really sorry. Damn, damn, damn! I knew I forgot something," Michael can only watch as his sister flips through picture after picture with tears streaming down her face.

"Two days here and I didn't even notice. I mean, they were everywhere, and not a single clue. God! How self-absorbed am I that I could even see that these were gone?" Emily continues going through the stack, an occasional smile breaking through her tears. "Oh, my God...Becca."

She gathers the photos together in a neatly packed pile, grasps them tightly, and brings them to her chest; her eyes closed in relief.

Some minutes had passed since the grandfather clock downstairs had struck midnight. Emily and Becca, decked out in crisp white, freshly laundered tanks and sweat bottoms, sat at Emily's open bay window, flicking ashes from their cigarettes into the night air. Ladytron played in the background as the girls looked down toward the ground two stories down. The yellow glow from the Wang's porchlight cast a hazy glow over the behemoth LTD in the driveway, as Bao leaped onto the hood, tail flicking, and then settling down into a comfortable position before a night of preening.

"Shit!" Emily exclaimed within the confines of a whisper. "No one let Bao in." She took another drag.

"Just grab him before we hit the sack. He looks pretty content where he is, anyway. Little, fat bastard." Becca sucked lightly on her Marlboro Light, pretending to inhale, spewing out more smoke than any pair of human lungs would willingly surrender. "Was he always that fat?"

Emily chuckled. "He was born fat. The fact that he sits on the dinner table while we eat doesn't help much either."

Becca's eyes widened. "Really? Māma Wang allows such a thing? Interesting. She won't let anyone get close to that table without anything less than a Silkwood shower."

"House rules don't apply to Bao, not when it comes to my Māma." Emily reached for the hard pack of cigarettes that rested between her legs and flipped the top, counting its contents. "One left. We'll have to share."

"Pass. This one's kinda stale, tastes funky." Becca took

one more drag and then dropped the flaming butt into her Diet Cherry Coke can. "Man, your mom really loves that cat. Frankly, I don't see it. What makes him so special?"

"He's a boy," Emily answered snarkily.

Becca chuckled and began to nod.

Emily held what was left of her cigarette out the window, as Becca poured a sad trickle of soda on the fiery tip, just enough to do the job and pull Bao's attention away from licking his paws for a second or two. "Now, now," Becca chuckled. "Don't get your dick in a twist."

Emily laughed.

Becca pulled her ponytail over her right shoulder, twisting its thick strands around her index finger. "God," she started, letting out a soft sigh. "Graduation's coming, and I still have no idea what I'm gonna do." Her eyes fixed themselves on Bao, below, and his sequence of comical rolls and stretches that unconsciously resulted in a shaking of her head. "That is one silly cat, Em."

"True that." Emily responded. "Anyway, you do know what you are gonna do. You are coming to USC with me. You got in. What's to worry about?"

Becca stared at Emily blankly, flipping her ponytail back over her shoulder. "I wish you would tell that to my parents then."

"I will."

"C'mon, Em, you know they already said no, plus they didn't really appreciate my applying without telling them...I told you they would freak, just like yours did."

Emily grabbed the pack, extended it toward her friend, and with a smooth slide of her thumb revealed the last remaining cigarette. "We are smoking the last one, dammit," she said with a tentative smile. "C'mon. Light 'er up."

Becca pulled the cigarette from the box and stuck it between her lips, then used the white lighter on the windowsill to get it going.

"They have to change their mind. They just have to. It's college for heaven's sake. Do they know what an opportunity this is?"

Handing the cigarette to Emily, Becca cocked her head and contorted her lower lip, releasing a slow-winding ribbon of yellow-gray smoke into her right nostril. She returned her head back to a normal angle, lips relaxed, and exhaled. "See that?"

"Something else Māma and Bàba Chen can be proud of. You're batting a thousand, sweetie."

Both girls let out soft giggles that trailed off into pensive looks.

"They know it's a big deal. Really, it's just that...we can't afford it. Not now with my mom's parents moving in with us." Becca's face was flushed, her eyes pulled away by the night sky. "It is what it is."

"Becca." Emily comforted, as she noticed the bitter aftertaste of stale tobacco on her tongue. "You never told me that. I mean, I know your grandparents moved in, but..."

"But they are family, so that is the end of that." Becca

took the cigarette with a forced smile and took a drag. "It's almost out." She took a slight drag before handing it back to Emily, who did the same.

The two blew smoke out the window, as Bao, who was now sitting on the hood, stared at them with a hint of judgment in his eyes.

Emily leaned forward, placing a hand upon Becca's. "Then I'm not going. We'll go to Saddleback and transfer out later, when things are different. Better. My Māma would just love that."

Becca smiled, squeezing Emily's hand. "No, we won't, but thanks for saying that anyway."

"I will stay. Los Angeles will be there a year from now, and—"

"And your mom will hate me more than she does now. She thinks I'm dragging you off as it is."

Emily rolled her eyes. "She doesn't hate you, Becca. Anyway, we'll see what happens. There is a whole summer ahead of us."

"Well, she doesn't seem to like me very much."

"She doesn't like anyone very much," Emily assured, fanning wisps of imaginary smoke out the window before closing it. "That's just her being her."

"She likes Bao." Becca smirked.

Emily chuckled. "Yeah, well, again...house rules."

Three evenly spaced coughs sounded from Emily's parent's bedroom across the hallway.

Becca's eyes widened. "Oh shit. Is that your mom?"

"Yup," Emily nonchalantly answered.

"Oh, my God. She knows we're up? That we're smoking?"

"Probably."

"Em!"

Emily swung her legs toward her bed and stood up. "Don't worry, she won't come in."

Becca just stared.

Emily headed toward her bed and pulled the pink bedspread, exposing the white, fitted sheet underneath. "She'll hang onto that until she can ambush me with it later."

"Well," Becca mused, "then we need to get a new pack tomorrow."

"Way ahead of you, bitch. Way ahead of you."

***

Pulled back to the present, Emily notices Michael standing in the doorway. "Why are these here? Who told you to get them out?" she asks.

For an instant, Michael is transported back a decade, to when nothing seemed quite as intriguing and mysterious as the closed door to his big sister's room. If he wasn't in there—when she was out of the house, of course—looking to discover all her deep, dark secrets, he was booby-trapping the place to remind her that he did, indeed, exist and was a force with which to be reckoned. He wants to speak and answer her question but knows it would cause more harm than good."

"Māma told you to get rid of these, didn't she?"

"To move them, Em. Don't make this out to be something it's not. She's just trying to make things less hard for you."

"And you're helping her," Emily accuses.

"I don't want to see you hurting either."

Emily takes the stack and carefully places it back into the box along with the rest of its contents and closes the lid flaps, then takes it to her mattress and rests it upon the extra pillow. "Mike, you all can't just erase things like that—from my life—because they're messy. I mean, I expect that bullshit from her...but you? You know how much Becca meant—means—to me, and you do this?"

Michael looks at his sister with a stoic expression and realizes he had jumped into an argument that could not be won. Emily's looking for a fight—not about stolen pictures, kitchen table criticisms, or unresolved teenage angst—and she's going to have it. "No one wants to see you hurting, Em," he declares, then walks away.

Emily drinks some more.

Christmas dinner is traditionally a seamless exercise in organization and routine. Guests are promptly seated at 8 p.m. with family members speedily transporting various porcelain bowls and platters of sides and meats from the kitchen to the dinner table. After all is brought out, Emily and Michael find their way to their pre-assigned seats. The room is lively with laughter and casual chatter that broaches varied subjects, such as Mr. Schwartz's never-ending tenacious battle with gout and Mr. Niedermeyer's yearly rant about increasing property taxes. Spirits are high and the mood of the room jovial save Emily's, who sits silently, barely acknowledging the celebratory vibration everybody else is immersed in. Strategically, she looks in one direction and smiles, then in another, and feigns laughter. Surrounded by family—by blood and extension—she can't remember ever feeling so alone. Much to her disappointment and shock, however, the table is set up with six chairs, not eight. The Chens are missing, and the volume of their absence falls hard up on her ears and mind. Michael leans over to his left and whispers, "You ok?"

"Never mind that," Emily answers under her breath. "Where are the Chens? Why didn't they come? They always come."

"Usually, yeah." Michael keeps his eyes peeled for his mother, who can smell upset like a rotten egg from across the house. "Māma gave me invitations for everyone here to hand deliver. Nothing for the Chens."

"What?" Emily blurts before she can adjust her volume accordingly. "She didn't invite them? That's insane, especially so soon after—"

"Look. You're gonna have to step your game up when Māma comes in. She'll see through this in a second."

"I don't know what you're talking about, Mike," Emily counters, still trying to wrap her head around her realization.

"Uh, when you turn to smile at someone, you actually need to look at them, so you don't smile like a freak at the back of their head. C'mon, sis. Sloppy work."

Emily takes great care to turn fully to her brother and lock eyes with him. *Smartass*, she subtly mouths.

"Maybe a shot would cheer you up?" he returns with a grin on his face.

Emily just glares, pretending not to know what he's alluding to.

"Bailey's," he mouths with a knowing look in his eyes.

Emily squints her eyes, follows with an obscure eye roll, and turns back around.

"Here comes the main course!" Mr. Wang announces from the kitchen. A reverent silence settles itself upon the dinner table along with the turkey somewhere between the green bean casserole and candied yams.

Emily looks down at her dinner plate, still annoyed, and realizes she's too intoxicated to eat.

"Well, Emily, being back must be quite the culture shock for you," Mr. Neidermeyer says. His tone is sincere. "Gotta expect that with your being away for so long. Well, I think we can forgive you for that. So good to have you back into the fold, again. Life seems to be treating you well. You faring well in the big city? Imagine that it can be 'dog eat dog' at times, no?"

"Things are good," Emily answers with an uncomfortable smile, grabbing a bottle of Pinot Noir from her brother. "Haven't been eaten yet." Pouring the rich-colored liquid into one of the very glasses she had washed that morning, she adds, "I am supposed to start a new position at the beginning of the year. More money, more responsibility. You know how that goes." She brings the glass to her lips and gives it a covert sniff to minimize any sign of wine snobbery, then takes a healthy mouthful.

"She is going to be the Director of Marketing at her agency—the youngest they have ever had. We are all very proud of her," Mrs. Wang clarifies, averting her eyes from Emily's embarrassed stare. "Very happy and very proud."

Emily peels her stare from her mother's cheek and gives Mr. Niedermeyer a smile. "Thank you for asking, Mr. Neidermeyer."

"What? What is that nonsense?" Mr. Neidermeyer poses in somewhat of a gruff manner. "Why we've known you since you were in elementary school, maybe a year or two before that. It was a long time ago, you understand. Time does quite a number on the memory. Plus, you're quite the successful, young lady now. Certainly, we can dispense with those silly formalities. Call us Dennis and Eileen. We insist." Mr. Neidermeyer gives the slab of turkey on his plate a couple of clumsy cuts with the edge of his fork and swirls the piece at its tip in the gory-looking mixture of mashed potato, gravy, and homemade cranberry sauce that makes his plate look like a scene of an accident. He crams the bleeding mass into his mouth and smiles; his wife, with a crown of Aqua-Net hardened silver locks nods excitedly to Emily, encouraging her. Emily smiles.

Mr. Schwartz, who has remained silent since the turkey hit the table, lifts his head from his plate and swallows the remnants of dry breast meat and half a dinner roll. "Yes, the Wang children are a remarkable lot. Why don't I think the store would do half as good if Michael weren't there? I don't know how you do it, son, with keeping things tight here at the house and all. You're taking those classes, too. Am I right?" he asks, shifting the spotlight.

"Yes, sir," Michael answers, lifting the napkin on his lap to dab gravy from the corners of his mouth. "I'm working on a Doctorate of Psychology, actually. It'll take a while, but I'm plugging along." Michael's eyes meet Mr. Schwartz's but don't linger long. "Things are going well. The courses are interesting, and I'm learning a lot." Micheal turns to Emily and asks her to pass the green bean casserole then quickly turns his focus back to the contents of his plate.

"My goodness!" Mr. Schwartz exclaims, a glass of wine in hand. "Quite the plateful you have there, son. How do you manage to get a graduate degree with that schedule of yours? Supporting your parents and all. Where do you find the time, much less the energy?"

Emily gives her brother a quizzical stare. "Supporting?"

Blushing, Michael slowly chews his mouthful of turkey leg. He swallows hard and gives his mouth another dab of napkin. "I don't know if it's all as impressive as that. I go part-time for now, just getting my feet wet, seeing how things go before I dive in. Besides, I drove myself pretty hard back in Manila. Don't want to burn myself out with the studying." Michael turns his face, slightly, in Emily's direction and gives it a subtle, dismissive shake.

"Well," Mr. Schwartz starts, as he grimaces, repeatedly rubbing his right knee, "you've impressed all of us regardless."

"Well, I don't know what John and Mary would do if you–" Mr. Neidermeyer starts to add, until his wife quietly places her right hand on his left, giving it a gentle squeeze. He pauses and raises his wine glass. "To Michael and Emily! Much happiness and success."

A collective "To Michael and Emily" rings out from around the table, as the two sit motionless, uncomfortable in their own skins but for very different reasons.

Emily grabs her wine glass, which had already seen three refills, and stumbles upward from her seated position. "I have a toast," she declares to the tops of everyone's head. Her announcement is met with stares and grins that hang in eager anticipation like goldfish awaiting a rain of Tetra flakes. "To Becca...and the Chens...who couldn't be here today...They are not far from our—well, my—thoughts. Merry Christmas!" She raises her glass and then gulps it down.

Like ice cream under a noon summer sun, the stares and smiles melt away. The silence–a deafening pall now– returns and emphasizes the rustle of every nervous shift and taps of wine glass bases descending upon the tabletop. Emily looks over at Michael, who glares at her, shaking his head. She then looks past him to the other end of the table at her father, who stares embarrassingly at his wife. He can't look at his daughter for fear of shaming his family and himself more than Emily already had. With slight hesitation, Emily's gaze turns to her mother at the opposite end of the table, where she sits, glass still raised, affect flat, and eyes boring through Emily's skull. "To Rebecca and the Chens," Mrs. Wang finishes with a strained smile. As she sets her glass down on the table, Mrs. Wang casts an emotionless glance at her husband that sends his eyes downward and tempers the fire in his gut.

"And what about the Chens, Māma?" Emily challenges. "Kinda strange they're not here. Why aren't they, exactly? On Christmas of all days, the first one without—"

"Well," Mrs. Wang coolly interrupts, "since this *is* their first Christmas without their daughter, the family decided to spend time together privately this year."

"Please. You didn't even ask them to come. You didn't even give Mike an invitation for them. Really, Māma, what is wrong with you?

"Oh, sweetie, you have things all wrong," Mrs. Niedermeyer contributes out of the blue, as she takes her wine glass. "Your mother called the Chens, while we were having coffee in the kitchen, to invite them days before you arrived, and they basically said, 'Thanks, but no thanks.' That poor family has been having such a hard time since October and pretty much keeps to themselves most of the time. I was surprised your mother even called since they have, basically, let everyone at church know they need space now more than anything." Mrs. Neidermeyer takes a sip from the glass, then another. "Still, she keeps reaching out. Always throwing lifelines, your mother, no matter what, but you can't help people who don't want it. Deserved...or not." She takes another sip with a slight hint of judgment in her eyes, scans the length of Emily's body, then grabs hold of her husband's hand and gives it a couple of firm squeezes.

Emily slowly sinks back into her chair, embarrassed and eyes glazed.

Stymied, Mr. Neidermeyer pauses to decode the message his wife was trying to send. He grabs his wine glass and gives it a quick toss back. "We've been so engrossed in this fine meal that I've completely lost track of time. You remember, sweetie," he says to his wife, clumsily trying to look natural. "We said we would help Father Singer take the haul from the blanket drive down to the homeless shelter tonight before mass?"

"You know, you're right. Completely went out of my head. I blame your cooking, Mary. Everything was just so...so good," Mrs. Niedermeyer praises with her voice trailing off. "We have to go, dear, but I will see John and you...hopefully at services tonight," Mrs. Neidermeyer insists, glancing at Emily and then at Mrs. Wang. "Or give me a call tomorrow when you have a chance." Both Neidermeyers rise and push their chairs in. "C'mon, David. Don't forget you said you'd give us a hand."

A forkful of stuffing and mashed potato still in Mr. Schwartz's mouth, a muffled *Wha?* escapes his lips, noticing that the two had already made their way to the front door and donned their coats. "But, I'm still eating," he says after swallowing.

"Yes, yes," Mrs. Neidermeyer says. "But we promised, and those blankets aren't going to make it into the homeless' hands by themselves."

"But, I'm still hungry."

"Oh, for goodness sake, you old fool, come get your coat! We can pick something up along the way."

Mr. Schwartz looks confused, and sighs. Turning to Mr. and then Mrs. Wang, he agrees, "Yes, now that I am chewing on it, I do recall saying I would help you with those sick children."

"Homeless," Mrs. Neidermyer sharply corrected.

"Yes, homeless." Mr. Schwartz empties his glass and gets up from the table. "Lovely dinner, Wangs. The best so far, I think. I'll see you soon, Michael. Lovely to see you again, Emily." He says as he clumsily makes his way backward to the foyer. "Always lovely to see you."

"Yes, that's lovely," Mrs. Neidermeyer assures the bumbling bookkeeper. "We'll talk tomorrow, Mary. Have a Merry Christmas everyone. Goodbye."

"Bye," the two men blurt out in unison before hurriedly following the dome of silver hair before them out the front door.

The Wangs sit in the dining room in silence, staring at

their unfinished plates, each wanting for words and a quick escape. The sudden monotonous chiming of the grandfather clock in the living room stabs the air, alerting everyone that it is now 9 p.m. mockingly, drawing attention to the vacuum that had swallowed the room, and everyone in it, whole. Emily brings her unsteady hand to the base of her empty wine glass and spins it clockwise with her fingertips. "Māma, I..."

"The dishes can wait until later. Your father and I are going to lie down for a while before church."

"Māma, please, I..." Emily pleads.

"I think it's been a long day for everyone, especially you and your brother. Cleaning and serving and all." Mrs. Wang looks at Emily's fingers that continue to spin the glass on the tabletop. "We could all use a chance to sleep it off."

"Really, Māma," Mike assures. "We can clear this mess. Won't take more than a few—"

"No," Mr. Wang interrupts. "Your mother is right. We have all had enough for tonight." He sits silently, looking at Emily as if she were a stranger. "More than enough."

Michael shrinks back further into his chair and stares at the bottle of Pinot Noir, wanting to take a swig.

"Māma? Bàba? I was upset and had a little too much to drink. It's no excuse, but I am sorry," Emily explains, dodging an audible scoff from her mother's end of the table. "I jumped to conclusions, and I shouldn't have. I am really, truly sorry for what I said. For what I—"

"Thought about me?" Mrs. Wang finishes. "Well, you

have made that quite clear." She whips the napkin off her lap and pats her forehead, moistened with beads of sweat, then her upper lip. With a flourish, equally as telling, she throws the white, square cloth upon her plate. "I don't know what your father and I have done, or what you think we have done to deserve this, but making a drunken fool of yourself solves nothing. I mean, bringing up The Chens like that...and Rebecca? None of this was about missing them; it was about you and how, yet again, nobody understands you or what you need. Well, you are not such a puzzle, Emily. You're not so complicated." Mrs. Wang gets up from her chair and firmly presses down the wrinkles on the front of her dress.

Emily, now speechless, pulls her hand back and places it back in her lap. "I was just so upset seeing all of Becca's stuff boxed up the way it was, like it was being discarded without a second thought. It felt hurtful, like you didn't even care how I might feel about it. Like you were just tossing her away because my grieving her is too inconvenient. Can you understand that?"

Mrs. Wang stops meddling with her dress long enough to bring her steely, dark eyes to Emily's. "I understand there is nothing convenient about any of this. Shaming the family in front of our friends. Using Rebecca's memory to humiliate me in front of everyone but insisting that *I* am some sort of monster. And the disrespect you've shown your father and I." She pushes her chair in and proceeds to walk toward the stairs, extending her hand toward her husband to accompany him up.

A churning in her stomach makes Emily want to vomit. Her face is flushed, and her head buzzes, either from all the alcohol or from the blunt force of the emotional hammer that had just come down upon everyone's head. Growing more uncomfortable with the surrounding silence, Emily turns to her father and apologizes. "I'm sorry, Bàba. We'll take care of the dishes and the kitchen." Emily feels Michael pinch her, hard, on her outer thigh, as Mr. Wang turns his eyes away and rises to join his wife.

"If it's convenient," Mrs. Wang pointedly says, disappearing from the dining room. Mr. Wang, shaking his head, follows right along with Bao, appearing out of nowhere, trailing behind in a slow saunter, but not before bidding the room adieu with a sassy flick of his tail.

Emily closes her eyes as if to wish the night away, leans back, and just breathes. She forgets the anger that had been gnawing at her all night and can only concentrate on the hurt and drama she had caused. Over and over, the same thought replies in her head: *How could I let this happen?*

"You shouldn't have come," Michael declares, breaking the silence.

"Not now, Mike. I feel bad enough already." Emily opens her eyes and gazes at the ceiling. "Everything is a mess; I don't need you to tell me that."

"You should have just stayed in LA. We would have all been better off."

Shocked by her brother's cold tone, Emily turns to him

and shakes her head. "Now you're laying into me? Great. Just great."

"You don't want to be here. We get it. Point made."

"You don't know what you're talking about."

"Don't I? You're just tolerating all of this—all of us. I mean you act as if you are doing us a favor by gracing us with your presence, but you're not. You're not even really here."

"Whatever," Emily says. "I am *here*. The folks expected me to come, so I came. It's not like I had much of a choice in the matter—neither of us does when they put their minds to something." Emily leans further back in her chair. "Heaven forbid I should miss Christmas at the Wang house."

"Lucky us," Michael jabs.

"What is your problem, Mike? I fucked up. I know that. I don't need your constant reminders of what a bitch I am."

"Oh, so you're aware. Well, I guess we can all rest easy then."

"Well, this is rich. You know how strict Māma can be when it comes to certain things. You've said so yourself. Becca's stuff packed away like that. She went too far."

"Sure, she can be a bitch, and infuriating—"

"See!"

"But I respect her enough to keep my opinions to myself," Michael says. "She didn't deserve this performance of yours tonight, especially in front of her friends. That was fucked, and you're fucked for doing it."

"Just shut up. You don't understand anything," Emily says. Her dismissive tone returns with a tinge of venom.

"I don't understand?" Michael chuckles. "Māma is right, you know. You're not that complicated. I mean, you're a smart girl, sis, but you're an easy read."

Emily glares. Michael continues.

"You're trying to sell everyone the idea that Māma is some cold, hard witch that could care less about you. That she is oblivious to feelings or just plain doesn't give a shit."

"She doesn't."

"But, the truth is that she's not the one you are mad at."

"Oh? Who am I mad at then, *Dr. Wang*?"

"Rebecca, for being drunk, for dying? The other driver for losing control of his car? Yourself…for not being here for her…like you'd always planned." Michael looks at his hands still clasped in his lap. "It wasn't your fault and certainly not Māma's. She just wants you to move on. Maybe she does push, but that's only because if she didn't, you'd drown in your self-pity. She's trying to help. If you would stop being judgmental for a minute, you'd see that."

"Wow, Mike. Impressive. Is that what you're learning at that online school of yours?" Emily says the words with the notion that they would somehow make her feel better, that seeing Michael gut-punched would make her feel less horrible, but she doesn't feel better or less horrible. Turning her face away, she begins to fidget in her chair. "I didn't come home for this shit."

Michael scoffs with a pained smile as he gets up from

his chair. "Well, home is in LA, isn't it?," he says, then heads to his room.

Emily sits alone in the dining room immersed in a stillness amplifying each of the racing thoughts spinning in her head. The acridness of her brother's words lingers in the air and tastes familiar. Despite the turn the evening had taken and the abandonment by her family, she feels like she could breathe again—an irony that does not escape her. She knows what Michael said was true. She was trying to hurt her mother for all the wrong reasons and ended up hurting everyone in the process. Through the quiet, she can hear the creaking of floorboards upstairs and the muffled sounds of tears, but she can't tell whose.

In her childhood bedroom, Emily looks at the clock. 3:08 a.m. and she hasn't slept. Reeling from the disastrous events of the evening, she finishes packing her bags with the knowledge that she will not return home for a while, maybe never. She places the last of her sweaters—her black, cashmere shrug that seems more like a shroud than a sweater—in her suitcase and shuts it, the clicks of the locks punctuating the end of a dark chapter in her life. She knows she should try to get some sleep, but the plan is to slip out before anyone wakes up, especially her mother, and drive back home. Staying awake seemed to be a logical course to take to avoid delaying her departure.

The ache in her stomach continues to nag her. She had sobered up some since dinner and determined that much of what she felt was due to hunger, not a lingering side effect of too much alcohol. She opens her door gingerly and quietly makes her way downstairs to the kitchen. Before her, she can see soft, yellow light trickling into the hallway from underneath Michael's door. It pains her to think of how she had hurt him earlier, and how she had belittled him for no good reason other than to make him feel as bad as she did. Emily stops at his door, her toes illuminated through the taupe-colored strands that bloomed from in between. She raises her right hand to knock, shifting her weight and causing the floorboards underneath her feet to creak. The light disappears with a muted click from the other side of the door. She still wants to knock but doesn't. She thinks, biting her lip, how wonderful it would be if erasing oneself was that simple. Gone with a *click*. At that moment, she realizes exactly how much she envied Michael, how much she always had.

The living room looks cold as she descends the staircase. Normally, the lights of the Christmas tree would be on, basking the room in random, warm splashes of red, yellow, blue, and green, scattering shadow from corner to corner, but the tree is dark. As Emily passes it on the way to the kitchen, she begins to feel overwhelmed by senses of loss and guilt. She enters the kitchen and reaches for the light switch to her right, and she notices a shadow-obscured form sitting at the table.

"Māma?" she says, straining her eyes for better focus. "Is that you?"

"What are you doing up?" Mrs. Wang answers softly.

Emily's eyes gradually adjust to the dark and reveal more of the room's surrounding details. "I couldn't sleep. I thought eating something might help."

"Yes, well," Mrs. Wang's eyes are focused on the lifeless tree in the other room. "There is plenty in the refrigerator."

"Yeah," Emily says as she casts her eyes downward to the floor. She grabs the refrigerator door handle and pulls it open to reveal shelves densely packed with dishes, meticulously wrapped in various festive colors of Saran Wrap. She is starving and wants to dive in; however, the thought of being the wrecking ball that plundered her mother's organizational artistry dictates otherwise. "Look, Māma, I—"

"There's a plate on the top shelf with white meat, no gravy. You'll have to eat it cold. The microwave is loud enough to hear upstairs and will wake your father and brother. Clean utensils are in the holder on the dish rack."

"You made me a plate?"

Mrs. Wang's glance shoots over to the illuminated figure of her daughter. "You can sit here. I was just leaving."

Emily closes the door and walks over to the table. Though the room is dark, she could make out subtle wisps of steam coming from her mother's mug of tea. "No, Māma. Don't leave...Dinner was awful. So was I. You don't deserve that. I don't know how else to say I'm sorry, but I am."

Mrs. Wang shifts in her seat as her eyes find their way down to a mug of tea. "Well, things are how they are."

"I just wanted to say that..."

"Before you left?"

"What?"

"You are leaving soon, no?"

Stunned, Emily pulls out a chair and sits down. "How do you—"

Mrs. Wang shakes her head. "I know because I know you, Lì. Things get messy, you run away. The more things change, the more they stay the same."

"I don't think that's fair."

"No," Mrs. Wang interrupts, "I am not criticizing. You *should* go."

"Māma." Emily's voice aches.

Mrs. Wang slowly pushes her mug forward and then gets up from her chair. She walks around to its back and clutches the top with her hands. "Your father and I will be fine. You shouldn't have said what you said to your brother though. He's a good man and kind. Too kind. He's sacrificed a lot to stay here and help us like he has and never complains, even though he could. Should."

"He told you."

"Of course. You hurt him."

"Māma, what are you talking about? I keep hearing about how much he helps, and how much the family owes him. What's going on?"

"We are getting older and managing things has become too much for us to do alone. Your brother is here, so he does what we can't."

"And Bàba? What's going on with him? The lawn. The

store being closed on Christmas Eve—one of its busiest days. What haven't you told me?"

Mrs. Wang hesitates and starts to spin her mug with her fingers. "He forgets things and gets confused. At first, small things that were easy enough to explain away, but now it happens more often and at work. It comes and goes, but it has made running Xiào Lì nearly impossible. Sometimes he forgets to reorder inventory. Sometimes he forgets how to run the register. There have also been a few times when he didn't even open it and went to the movies instead or slipped into the garage to just sit."

Emily's eyes begin to tear as she hears her mother's words and images of her father's face from the night before flash across her mind. "I'm so sorry. I didn't know. Why didn't you all tell me you were in trouble, that you needed help?"

"What purpose would that serve? You are doing so well...with so much still weighing you down. You think you resent us now, just imagine if you were dragged back here."

Emily remains silent.

"It pains us to see how much Michael sacrifices. It would have been nice to have you closer, to help, but life—and your happiness—had other plans for you. We know that. Still, sometimes it's hard to accept when things don't work out the way you want them to...I think you're starting to learn that, no?

"Still, you should have said something. This isn't fair to Michael."

"No, it isn't. We know he would like to go off on his own, like you, but he's agreed to stay, and we are grateful for that. Being part of a family comes with prices, as well as gifts, Lì. I don't know that you ever fully grasped that." Mrs. Wang grabs her mug pours its contents out into the sink. She looks out of the window into the blackness and fights back the urge to cry. "Eat something and go to bed. I will wake you in a few hours." She turns and ekes out a smile that looks more like a grimace. She walks around Emily, placing her hand on her daughter's left shoulder as she passes by.

"I can stay," Emly declares.

"No. You shouldn't." Mrs. Wang says. "You should go home and live the life you've been blessed with. Be grateful. You do need to talk to someone, Lì. Let go of whatever it is that weighs you down so. Father Singer suggested a grief group, perhaps at a church back home. Just get help somewhere." She pulls her hand away and leaves the kitchen as silent as it was when Emily first walked in.

Emily sits in the dark of the kitchen long after her mother leaves. The comfort of being alone, which had once given her a sense of calm, has become smothering and hard to bear. She looks down at the plate before her that was still tightly wrapped in plastic and feels sick at the thought of it. Emily wants to cry but can't.

Before going upstairs to get what little sleep she can before heading out, she takes the plate and brings it back to the refrigerator. In vain, she gives the appliance's contents one last look though she knew fully well that she couldn't manage to eat a thing. In the back, she notices an unopened, brown bottle of Bailey's tucked away between a green, plastic Tupperware bowl of mashed potatoes and dinner rolls wrapped in foil. She shuts the refrigerator door with a good slam and stands before the humming goliath, shaking her head. "Fucking duwendes."

Part 2

Written by Alexandra Naughton

It's early evening, that space of time between supper and twilight when an essence of something unnamable and unseeable engorges the atmosphere with embryonic magic and makes even the most ordinary occurrences seem otherworldly. Magical and otherworldly, that is, unless you're being dragged by your dogmatic mother to a grief group in the basement of a church.

Emily sits on a folding chair in a circle of folding chairs. Hands folded, her face puffy and unexpressive, passively listening to a woman two seats down from her drone about missing her border collie who died after eating one of the many poisoned meatballs some creep had been leaving in the public parks of Aliso Viejo. The idea of a dog-hating pet killer lurking in the bushes and leaving behind toxic treats for unsuspecting canines is somewhat interesting, but Emily's too distracted by a headache and the rage shouting at her behind her eyes at a low and constant volume to really register what is being said in the room.

Her mother had dropped her off with a warning. While Emily feels resentful of the implication of needing a support group, it seems like the least she can do after ruining yet another family holiday with an intoxicated meltdown. If Emily was waiting for rock bottom, she's surely hit it now. Becca is dead, and Emily is living a life haphazardly designed by her own turmoil. What was once a promising career is now over. Her boss finally had enough of Emily missing meetings and showing up late reeking of vodka and vomit, if she bothered to show up at all. Emily's performance and behavior had gotten so out of control she's been designated an 'unhireable' via the gossip grapevine to other advertising agencies in Los Angeles. She has no hope of restarting somewhere else. At least locally. Becca is still dead, and Emily is living with her parents again after trashing her apartment, neglecting to pay bills, and getting evicted. It took a month of moping around her parents' house while she detoxed and applied for temp jobs to finally get dumped here. "Get it together or else," her mother had said. Or else what?

The woman mourning her border collie finishes her sob session and the grief group leader calls for a break. Needing a stretch and maybe some sugar, Emily wanders over to the refreshment buffet. She looks over the Costco pastry spread on the folding table and decides against it, opting for just a cup of coffee. She presses down on the coffee dispenser and feels a short wave of shock roll over her as a hand softly touches her shoulder and a voice behind her says "First time?" Emily turns around and looks up to the polished and professional-looking woman awaiting her attention. With her shiny black hair, silk suit, and Louboutin pumps, she looks like a flash-forward version of Emily had she not imploded her career and her life. The version Emily could have been if her Becca hadn't been stolen from her. Emily shakes off the thought and shrugs in response to the woman's question.

"I'm Monica," the woman says, offering her hand. Her

face looks gentle and kind. Open, like a receiver of secrets. Like her forehead wouldn't start twitching if she heard some of the really gnarly stuff Emily hasn't been able to share with anyone, let alone admit to herself. Emily stares at Monica's face for a heavy moment, then reaches her hand out for a firm shake. "Emily," she says. Her voice is crunchy from not having spoken since before getting dropped off. There is a pause between them as they study each other.

"The cookies are stale, but I like this church," Monica says, watching Emily's eyes. "I love all the original artwork on the walls down here."

"The murals? Yeah they've looked that way since I was a kid," Emily says.

"Great use of chiaroscuro," Monica says.

Emily raises her eyebrows quickly, then frowns. "What about you," Emily says. "Was this your first time? You didn't share either."

"Oh, I come and go to these things all over the place. I don't always share but I like to listen."

Emily blows on her coffee, sips, then regrets it. "But you've lost someone too," Emily says.

Monica moves her mouth to begin to speak but stops herself. "Many years ago, yes."

"You don't like to talk about it, do you?"

"It doesn't come up a lot, but I think about him all the time."

"Does it get any easier?" Emily asks.

"You get used to it. Your loss is recent, I assume?"

Emily looks away and stares ahead toward one of the wall murals depicting children holding hands and walking in a circle in some sort of ceremony. Emily is looking at nothing, tucked away in a memory of Becca in grade school sharing the second cupcake in her pack of two during lunch time. She focuses on one of the painted children, a brown skin girl with purple pigtails and closed eyes as if remembering something fondly. To ground herself, Emily touches the chain of the necklace around her neck and comes back to the present.

"Yeah," Emily says. "I've been having a hard time with it. My mother is about to disown me with how I've been reacting."

"Would she really disown you?"

"She might this time. I've pushed her to her breaking point. We've always butted heads, but neither of us were prepared for this. I've become the embodiment of my family's shame."

"The first few months can be really tough," Monica says. "If you let me, I know I can help you."

"Help me how? Are you a therapist?"

"Sort of, but not really. What I provide is more of a holistic approach than traditional therapy. Do you have some time tonight to sit down with me and discuss more? It won't take too long."

"I'm not sure," Emily says, taking a step backward, nearly bumping into the refreshment table.

"What if I told you that in thirty minutes flat we can get

to the root of the problem and get your mother off your back? That's why you're here, right? She forced you here?"

Emily clears her throat. "Okay, I think I can do thirty minutes."

"Great," Monica says. "There's a coffee shop not far from here. Did you drive?"

"I'm not allowed to drive right now. Māma dropped me off."

"My Audi's out front," Monica says. "I can drop you back here once we're done."

At the diner down the road, Emily sips from her cup. Having recounted everything that's led her up to here, the events from the past three months of her life, her mistakes and worries and all the things she blames herself for. It felt good to say out loud, to be listened to patiently and undistractedly, but now she feels raw, like her body is stinging and cold after the outer layers of her skin had been sloughed off. As she self-consciously uncrosses her leg and recrosses with the other leg on top, she feels Monica eyeing her from across the table. To take the attention off herself, she begins her own line of questioning.

"When did you decide to move to San Francisco?" Emily asks.

Monica grins, then looks down. "I didn't think about it, I just did it. Casey gave me an opportunity to leave my job and start something great from the ground up. I haven't looked back once."

"Did it help to live in a new place?"

"You take everything with you. Whether you know it at first or not."

"Wherever you go, there you are."

"Yes, and I was prepared for that. I didn't think I'd be running away from my old life. I knew it was coming with me. But I guess yeah, it did help to have a new routine, new distractions. A reason to make new memories in a new setting. And it is a beautiful setting. Have you ever been?"

Emily swallows hard. "No, but we talked about going. Me and Becca, when we were in high school."

"But you never did?"

"We wanted to go to college there. The University of San Francisco, it's a Jesuit school. I actually thought Māma would be on board because of that. But it was too far away."

"I think you're going to love it there."

Emily sits stunned for a moment, shakes her head to make sure her ears are working.

"What do you mean?" Emily asks.

"Well, I want you to come work with us. You're a natural."

"Natural?"

"You can read people. You have an instinct for what people are hiding and you know how to get it out of them. You read me dead to rights."

"And you want me to come work for you?"

"Not for me. With me. We're building Fiducia and making it national. We've already got some offshoot centers in different parts of California and Colorado, but the next step is to really spread out. And I know you can help with that. I mean. If you want to."

"Just like that?"

"Just like that."

"What am I going to tell my mother?"

"You're gonna tell her what you need to tell her. That you've recognized what you've done, that you are taking responsibility for your past actions—"

"And I want the chance to make it up to her."

"Right. I'll send you an email tonight with more information about the role and the salary and benefits. I don't need an answer right away, so you can take your time and think about it."

"Well, I'm definitely interested. We should probably head back to the church. I want to get there before Māma does."

Monica pulls a twenty out of her wallet and lays it on the table. "Let's get out of here."

***

The early 20th-century ten-story flatiron building where Fiducia has made their home and headquarters stands looming over the financial district in downtown San Francisco. A steely gray sky hovers above as a chilling wind rips through the tunnels created by the surrounding concrete structures.

It's a Sunday and the area is dead, aside from a few

straggling tourists making their way to and from the hotels of Union Square and the waterfront. A pigeon flaps its wings and waddles a little path on the sidewalk, stopping at Emily's feet. She looks down at the bird gaping up at her. It blinks then flies off.

"It was previously occupied by 'dot-com era' startups and boutique travel service companies, but once Casey Abnehmer set his sights on it, he had to have it," Monica says, holding the front door open for Emily.

They step into a beautiful lobby: high vaulted ceilings, art deco chandeliers, intricately tiled floors with central mosaics leading to a seating area and fountain featuring a statue of a woman holding a bowl over her head. Water trickles from her overflowing vessel.

"So, what happened, did those other businesses just leave, or did they get bought out?" Emily asks.

Monica raises her hand and pinches her fingers and thumb into a finger purse gesture. "He made them an offer they couldn't refuse," she says.

"You're kidding," Emily says.

"Only sort of," Monica says, pressing the elevator up button. "He got the building management company in a conference room and did a demo of one of our courses. After that, they agreed to sell him the building and relocate the tenants."

They step into the elevator.

"That's incredible," Emily says.

"Casey is a very interesting human. You'll see. Just

remember to assert yourself and speak your mind. That's how you win him over. Oh, and don't forget to refer to him as Cipher."

"Cipher, right," Emily says.

The elevator doors close and a wave of trepidation hits Emily with full force. She clasps her hands together and looks up at the ceiling of the elevator to count the mirror tiles above them. Her reflection stares back at her for a second and Emily stifles a laugh. "Just relax, stay open," she reminds herself in her head.

"I'll take you to your locker first," Monica says and enters a code into a panel by the door, then hits the button for the second floor.

"I get a locker?" Emily asks.

"Yep, we all do. For our jackets and bags, and more importantly our watches and phones. When we're in the building we need to stay mindful and present, and that means no digital distractions."

"That's so retro," Emily says.

They step off the elevator and Emily's nostrils are assaulted with the scent of lemon Pine Sol. She follows Monica down a long dimly lit corridor with rows of lockers on either side, the long skinny ones that you'd see in a high-school hallway.

"It's essential to our practice. If you need a computer for lesson planning or printing out packets, you can always go to the fifth-floor library. Here, 256, this one is yours."

Emily opens the locker and slips her things inside. "No

lock?"

"That's right, we don't lock them. We're supposed to be able to trust everyone here."

Emily nods. They head back to the elevators.

"By the way, the elevator code is 10151000. You'll need that in order to leave the lobby and to move between floors. Stairs are for emergencies only; an alarm will sound if a door to the stairwell is opened."

The rules seem stricter than Emily imagined, but it must be for a good reason. She decides not to question it too much.

Once the elevator doors open at the tenth floor, Emily and Monica step out to see Casey Abnehmer waiting for them in the conference room. He's shorter than Emily pictured, and softer, with curly blonde hair, a small potbelly, and a clean shaved face. From everything Monica had told her, she imagined Casey as some macho frat boy type, hyped and muscular and ready to play beer pong while totally controlling the spotlight. Not this doughy baby face.

"It's so great to meet you, Emily. I've heard wonderful things," Casey says, getting a hold of Emily's hand and shaking it with both of his own. His hands are warm and smooth. The kind of hands that are exempt from doing household chores.

The conference room is the entire level. Floor-to-ceiling windows line the perimeter. A gigantic rectangular table with rolling office chairs rests ominously in the center of the room. On the side of the room opposite the elevator doors is a platform stage with a whiteboard, a microphone stand, and a bucket of tennis balls.

"It's so nice to meet you, too. That's quite a handshake you've got there, Cipher," Emily says.

"We believe it's important to convey our openness and community mindedness with a warm and welcoming handshake," Casey says. "It's your only chance to make a lasting first impression and assert your dominance."

"That makes a lot of sense," Emily says. "I know it's too late to give you a first impression of me, but can we try again anyway?"

Casey looks over at Monica and Monica just nods. Casey looks back at Emily. "I knew I was going to like you. Of course we can try again."

Emily steps with her right foot toward Casey, cocks her wrist downward accepting his hand, and covers the clasp with her left hand. They shake hands for a moment maintaining eye contact until Emily loosens her grip.

"Take a look at this one!" Casey says. "Way to assert your dominance. I love it."

"I want to get her set up to start teaching soon," Monica says. "But we need to discuss territory."

"Let's do that over dinner. I want her out in the field as soon as possible," Casey says. "I need you to set up materials for tonight's seminar. I'll give this one a tour in the meanwhile."

"Sure thing, boss," Monica says, unpacking her briefcase onto the conference room table.

Casey puts his arm around Emily and guides her toward the elevators. "So, what has Monica told you about me? Did she mention that I live in the basement? She loves telling all the pretty new recruits about basement-dwelling-Casey."

"I did not!" Monica calls out.

"I kid, I kid," Casey says, leading Emily onto the elevator. Emily turns her face and gives Monica a sheepish smile as the elevator doors close.

***

The third floor of Fiducia's HQ is where staff eat their meals and out of town members hang out in between training modules. The open plan layout is inviting and set up in such a way to encourage conversation and connection, full of plush couches and chairs, floor pillows and coffee tables, and folding cafeteria tables often seen in public school lunchrooms.

"I got those at an auction," Casey says, pointing at the lunch tables where several other members are eating bowls of soup. "I love auctions. It's like gambling, but with a greater reward to risk ratio."

"We had the same tables at my high school," Emily says.

"When I saw them, I had to have them," Casey says. They serve as a reminder that we're all still students. We all have more to learn. Are you hungry?"

"I could eat," Emily says.

"Well let's get you a little something, then we can sit, and you can meet some of the Sodales," Casey says, directing Emily toward the kitchen.

"Sodales?"

"Didn't Monica tell you? That's what we call the top recruiters here. They're not people who have just taken a few courses. Sodales are fully devoted to our cause, and they're helping us change the world."

"I want to change the world," Emily says.

"I can tell, and I think you will."

"What can I get for you, Cipher?" A kitchen worker asks when Casey and Emily reach the kitchen window.

"This is Emily, she's our new shining star," Casey says. "Can you get her a bowl of what everyone else is having?"

"Sure thing. Nice to meet you, Emily," the kitchen worker says.

"Nice to meet you, too. What's your name?" Emily says.

"I'm Robert, but you can just call me Chef. That's how I like to be known. I trained at Le Cordon Bleu before I came here," he says, handing Emily a bowl of something gray and creamy. "Mushroom."

"Looks good. Thanks, Chef," Emily says as she walks away, being guided again by Casey over to the cafeteria tables. As they approach the tables, the seated members, dressed in black and gray business attire, stand and bow at Casey who smiles and waves his hand, urging them to sit again and pay him no mind. Using his hand on the small of her back, he takes Emily over to an unoccupied table where

Casey can semi-privately continue his spiel.

Before Emily can raise her spoon to take the first sip of the soup, Casey pulls a deck of tarot cards seemingly out of nowhere. "I'll let you meet the others in a moment, but do you mind if I give you a three-card reading? It won't take long."

Emily raises her eyebrows. "I don't know if I believe in this stuff."

"What's to believe? It's all up to your own interpretation. Tarot is simply another tool to help unlock the massive amount of data we already have stored within ourselves."

"What do I have to do?"

Casey shuffles the cards. "Imagine a question you want answered. Don't tell me what it is. Just think about it and shuffle these three times."

Emily takes the cards and shuffles them, then hands them back to Casey.

"Good. Now let's see what the cards say."

The first card depicts a big red heart with three swords pierced through the middle. In the background rain clouds storm, pouring heavy droplets.

Emily gasps lightly.

"The first card is your past. Three of Swords," Casey says. "This card represents grief, loss, heartbreak, trauma. Is that bringing up anything for you?"

She nods her head.

"These things happen every day," Casey says. "People

get dumped, they lose a family member, they miss out on an opportunity. But these are all lessons. It's not just pain, it's a chance to learn something about yourself and how you face challenges."

He leans back with his arms behind his head. "When we're confronted with a difficult circumstance we're being presented with the chance to get stronger and smarter and more attentive because of it. We're finding meaning within ourselves, and within the world. The curtain is opening for you. You're set to start the next stage of your life. And the director is telling you to move forward and don't look back."

That's just a coincidence, Emily thinks.

"I can tell that this is resonating," Casey says. "Okay, now flip the second card."

Emily reaches her right hand from her lap and turns the second card over.

"Is it upside down?" Emily asks.

"Yes, we call that a reverse card," Casey says, turning the card and pushing it toward Emily so she can better see the details on the card.

"This one's very busy, visually," Emily says.

"The meaning of the reverse card is different from the upright card. Kind of like a mirror image."

"Chiral."

On the card, a shadowy figure of a person stands in the foreground turned toward a swirling gray cloud looming ahead. Bursting from the cloud are seven gold goblets, each overflowing with their own unique offering. One has a snake slithering out, another has a mound of baubles scooped into it like gaudy ice cream.

"Gifts and curses," Casey says. "This is the Seven of Cups."

A woman wearing a gray pencil skirt and matching gray blazer approaches the table holding a clipboard. She looks at Casey, then looks down at her feet.

"This card represents choices," Casey says, ignoring the woman with the clipboard, "and in your case, since the card is reversed, a feeling of being overwhelmed by choices. Are you the type of person who has a hard time making decisions?"

"Not usually," Emily says.

The woman with the clipboard continues to wait silently as Casey describes the Tarot card's significance to Emily. Despite listening intently, Emily can't stop looking over to the waiting woman with her peripheral vision.

"I see you, Cheri," Casey says, not breaking his eye contact with Emily. "What do you want?"

The woman looks up and over at Casey. She adjusts the bun atop her head and speaks quickly, with a nervous energy. "I'm so sorry to interrupt you, Cipher. There's someone waiting for you in the lobby." She blinks twice and looks as if she's about to speak again, but Casey cuts her off.

"Is this something that you can't handle yourself?" Casey says, winking at Emily. Cheri, turning red-cheeked, looks over at Emily, then looks down at her feet again.

"I tried, Cipher, but he won't leave. He's insistent that

he sees you today. He has a document," Cheri says. Her eyebrows jolt up and down, almost nudging Casey.

"Take a photo of him and tell him to wait in the lobby."

Casey shakes his head as Cheri turns and heads for the elevators. "She's a good assistant, very devoted to me, but sometimes she just doesn't think."

Casey stands and starts gathering the tarot cards. "We'll have to finish this another time," he says before walking off.

Emily stands, looking confused. "Thank you for the reading," she says, but it's unclear if he hears her.

"Why don't you come join us?" a voice behind her says. Emily turns to the group of people sitting a few tables down.

"Hi, I'm Emily," she says, walking over and sitting down with the bowl of soup she still hasn't gotten a chance to taste.

"We know who you are," a man wearing khakis and a light gray collared shirt says. "We've read your file. I'm Stu." He extends his hand and Emily firmly shakes it, using both of her hands. "And this is Donna, and George."

Emily shakes Donna and George's hands. "I can see you've already got the handshake down," Donna says.

"Practice makes perfect," Emily says.

"How are you finding things so far?" George asks.

"I think things are never what they seem, but I'm happy to be here," Emily says, finally raising the spoon to her mouth to try the mushroom soup. "Oh, this is delicious."

"You're ready to turn your life around, right?" Donna asks.

"Something like that. How long have you guys been members?"

A chime sounds over the PA system. Stu, George, and Donna all stand. "We're actually Sodales," Donna says.

"We've been here for years, but not as long as Monica," Stu says. "Anyway, we'll see you around. It's study time."

"Study time?" Emily asks, following the group toward the elevators.

"We don't wear watches," George says, "but our time is still highly regimented. The chimes let us know when it's time to move on to the next agenda item. You'll see."

The elevator doors open and Monica steps out. "See you later," Stu says as the elevator doors close.

Monica approaches the table. "Oh good, I'm glad you're still here," she says to Emily. "Did you eat?"

"Not really, I just started."

"Where did Casey go?"

"He was reading my tarot cards, but Cheri told him someone was waiting in the lobby. It seemed important."

"That's odd. He doesn't usually get unscheduled visits from outsiders."

"The vibe was odd, for sure."

"Don't worry about it. Let's take a walk and I'll show you my favorite French bakery, it's not far. Then we can swing by the fifth-floor library and get your reading materials. You're going to need to do a lot of reading in the next few weeks to get you completely up to speed."

"That's not a problem."

"Good. Now tell me, do you like caneles?"

***

It doesn't take long for Emily to get acclimated with Fiducia. The reading is intense, but she loves the ritual of studying and taking notes. When your final project is yourself, there's always improvements to be made.

The apartment Monica helped her move into gets great light. The space is roomy and cozy, and steps away from Dolores Park. In terms of size and modern appliances, it's a slight downgrade from her old place, but since Fiducia owns the building, she's living rent-free.

Emily was great at her old job that was able to pay for her old place, but she had grown to hate everything about her old life. Her old job was an escape. A way to stay busy, a way to stay away from her family. Away from any other people. She was always working and busy, but she wasn't actually living.

In the three months since she joined Fiducia, Emily has been hard at work coaching, writing lessons, studying, and completing certifications. She's already moved up in rank and earned three green ribbons which she's showcased above the defunct fireplace in her apartment. Her new life has meaning.

When she's not at HQ or sleeping, she's out and about, going to mixers, conventions, and tech industry events looking for new recruits. She's proven to be a quick study, and Monica has taught her a lot: how to spot the type of people who would be most open to the kind of help Fiducia provides, how to convert those who are a bit tougher to crack, how to put an idea in someone's head and get them to make the decision you want them to make while making it seem like it all came from them, how to challenge someone's language to find out what they're holding back. She's doing things she never thought she'd be able to do.

When she wakes up every morning just before dawn, she showers and dresses, then sits in her living room to meditate and catch up on her readings. When 7 a.m. rolls around, she puts on her light jacket and walks through the park to get coffee at a cafe nearby where she's already recruited three baristas and four regular customers to take an introductory course with Fiducia.

"I'm breathing with my whole belly," this morning's barista says to Emily as she walks over to the counter to get her usual latte.

"Is it helping?" Emily asks.

"You know, I didn't think it would at first, but I do feel this immense clarity in my day to day now."

"I'm so happy to hear that."

"Do you think I can have a session with you sometime this week, maybe tomorrow? I want some feedback on the letter to my former self."

"I would love to! I should have some time, but can you check my Calendly and grab a slot?"

"Thanks, it would be really helpful. I'm tripping up on

the 'forgiving transgressions' part and want to make sure I'm giving myself the right directives."

"That part can be tricky," Emily says and sips her latte.

"Thanks again, I'll pick a time and see you tomorrow."

"Sounds good. We can meet at the same bench."

At HQ, Monica grabs Emily's arm as she's waiting for the elevator. "I'm so proud of you, you've really been crushing it since you got here," Monica says.

Emily laughs. "You know, before I got here, I was worried about not fitting in, but I've been so busy with teaching and the coursework that I haven't had time to remember to worry."

"What's there to be worried about? Everyone here loves you. Casey especially. He told me he knew you would do good things for Fiducia the moment he laid eyes on you."

"Really?"

"Don't be self-limiting. You're helping us change the world."

"I'm trying, I know that much."

"That's all we can do. What do you have going on today? I want you to come with me to Menlo Park."

The elevator doors open, and several other members step off. Monica and Emily step out of the way but don't get on.

"You mean, for Facebook?"

"Yes. I'm doing upper-level executive coaching this week and I think it would be good for you to attend. Besides, I could use your help."

"I'm flattered. What would you need me to do?"

Monica pulls out her car keys from her purse and jingles them. "Why don't we just talk about it on the drive over? If I didn't think you could handle it, I wouldn't even ask."

Emily gulps, then takes a deep breath through her belly. "I'll move my appointments to tomorrow. Let's do it."

"Just text Cheri. She can adjust your calendar. Now let's go, I'm parked around the corner."

***

Monica and Emily cruise south on US-101, hitting some traffic but nothing out of the ordinary for a Bay Area commute. Emily gazes out at the long line of cars ahead moving about as quickly as she can jog. A smile crawls above her chin, but she quickly suppresses it.

"I like that look on your face," Monica says. "What do you want to ask me?"

Emily laughs and looks over at Monica in the driver's seat, steadily maneuvering the Mercedes G Wagon with one hand on the steering wheel. Her other hand holds a lit cigarette which she occasionally puffs and flicks ashes from out the open window.

"Does my face betray me that much?"

"To anyone else, probably not. But I know your tells. Do you want to know if we're going to meet Mark?"

"The Zuck man. Yeah, the thought did cross my mind."

"He was one of my first big clients. My one-on-ones with him years ago are the reason I've gotten so many ribbons. We'll probably not see him today, but he's been a huge influence in spreading our message around Silicon Valley and getting his whole company through training. I've already worked with the board of directors and the C-suite."

"Who are we meeting with today?"

"Today we're going to be working with the marketing and operations teams."

"So, corporate intro, followed by a breakout sesh and vision mapping?"

"Yes, exactly, then later we'll have a catered lunch and some hot seat training."

"Full day."

"Well, you know these guys help pay the bills. Gotta make the most of it."

***

Emily walks from the back of the room down the aisle between rows of folding chairs where other marketing and operations team members sit silently. Some of them look bored but the majority look nervous, knowing that they might be asked to sit on the hot seat next.

"I'm scared," a marketing manager says, sitting on a stool at the front of the room. A name tag sticker is stuck over the pocket of his polo shirt. "Bill" is his scribbled name.

"What are you scared of?" Emily asks.

"Failing, I guess," Bill says, looking down at his feet.

"Are you afraid of failing, or are you afraid of trying?"

The room is quiet as Bill mulls over the question. "I never thought of it that way before," he says.

"Okay, now close your eyes and imagine for a moment with me," Emily says. "A large wheelbarrow is rolled to your front door. I want you to visualize filling the wheelbarrow with apples. Can you do that for me?" She opens her hypothetical question to the crowd. "In fact, can everyone in the room please close your eyes and imagine that you're filling a wheelbarrow with apples?"

Emily looks over at the rows of Facebook employees sitting before her with their eyes closed. She smiles quickly, pleased with herself, then reasserts herself with a serious look.

"Can you tell me what the apples look like, Bill?" she asks.

"They're green and shiny, with brown stems," Bill says.

"Good. Now I want you to empty the wheelbarrow. Dump all those apples out onto the ground and fill the wheelbarrow with your fear."

Bill's eyebrows furrow, apparently struggling with this visualization exercise.

"I can't," Bill says.

"Anyone else?"

The room is silent. A few people shake their heads.

"Fear is this intangible thing, right? It's anxiety activated by the primal part of our brains that's supposed to keep us safe from apex predators, like wolves and bears," Emily says. "Fight, flight, or freeze. Except, unless you're Grizzly Man, people today don't really have the everyday worry about being mauled to death while collecting berries in the forest. Instead, we fear fucking up. Missing our impending deadlines, not making our quotas, not keeping our bosses happy."

Late afternoon sunlight spills into the room through the large windows of the westward side of the building. Emily faces the windows and closes her eyes, feeling the warmth spread over her face. "You all can open your eyes now," she says. "Everyone take a deep breath with me. Let's stand up and stretch for a moment."

The sound of chairs scraping the tile floor fills the room as the Facebook employees take to their feet and raise their arms above their heads.

"Breathe in a deep breath," Emily says. "Start all the way from your belly. If it helps, hold your belly with both hands and breathe in. Feel the air press up through your belly to your chest to your neck. Then hold it and breathe out through your nose."

The whole room breathes in and out in soft unison, like separate pipes on an old church organ taking in air then releasing it in one long note.

"It feels good to be in your own body," Emily says, walking around the room and stopping to touch the shoulder of a Facebook employee who looks like they're on the verge of tearing up. "It feels good to remember that you're in charge of your body. You're in charge of whatever impulses your brain is trying to feed you. You can regulate all of it. You just need to stand up for yourself. Fear is completely useless. It doesn't drive us to do better. It keeps us from being our best selves. Failure is essential. We learn something new about ourselves and our environment every time we fail."

Monica, standing at the back of the room like a proud parent at her child's dance recital, gives Emily a nod of approval.

"Let's all close our eyes again. Now tell me, Bill. Can you locate where the fear is inside your body?"

"Yeah," Bill says. "It's in my chest, stuck in my lungs."

"Is fear doing anything for you? Is it helping you by existing in your lungs?"

"It's not."

"What about you, Melissa," Emily says to another Facebook employee. "Can you pinpoint where the fear lives inside of you?"

"It's in my throat," Melissa says.

"And is it helping you by staying in your throat?" Emily asks.

"Definitely not," Melissa says.

"I want everyone to locate where their fear and anxiety lives. Once you've found its hiding spot, raise your hand."

Slowly, everyone in the room raises a hand.

"Okay, good. Now, imagine a bright white light shining its brilliance into that hiding spot and chasing the fear away, chasing it out of your body and removing it. Now repeat after me: I am bigger than my fear."

"I am bigger than my fear."

"I am in control of my body."

"I am in control of my body."

"I can accomplish the tasks I set out for myself."

"I can accomplish the tasks I set out for myself."

"Failure is just a new beginning."

"Failure is just a new beginning."

***

Back at HQ that night, Monica leads Emily up to the penthouse conference room where 50 other Fiducia members are waiting with a cake. Casey is seated in an armchair on the stage. He stands and starts clapping as Monica and Emily enter the room, which prompts the rest of Fiducia members to turn their attention to Monica and Emily and also start clapping.

Emily looks at Monica and gives her a hug. "Congratulations!"

"It's not for me! I made a call when you were doing your hot seats with the Facebook gang. Go on up there and get your green ribbon!"

Emily covers her mouth with a hand but composes herself and hugs Monica again. "This is so unexpected," she says.

"But so, deserved. You're ready to start leading your

own corporate summits. Now come on, I'll walk with you up to the stage."

Feelings of shock and excitement vacillate through Emily's body as she approaches the stage, and her deep belly breaths and other grounding techniques, like taking a mental inventory of objects in the room and their corresponding colors, aren't helping so much. She feels like she's floating on a cloud, as if she's barely in control of her legs as she climbs the two short steps to the platform where Casey stands and is still clapping. Cheri appears from Emily's right side and slips a green sash over her head.

Casey raises a hand in the air, signaling for everyone to quiet down and get seated. After the attention is back on him, Casey embraces Emily then raises her arm and spins her as if they're dancing together.

"Just look at you," he says to Emily, but also to the whole room. "We're all so proud of you. Aren't we? Let's give Emily another round of applause."

The members stand again and clap their hands. Monica, also standing on the stage which Emily just noticed, shouts out a few cheers and gives her a thumbs up.

"We're all hustlers here," Casey says. "You wouldn't be here if you weren't. We've all made it as far as we have because we believe in Fiducia, and we believe in the mission. We all know our purpose and what it means to live a more principled life. And the way that we help ourselves grow and learn is by spreading our mission and teaching others to lead more principled lives. And when we see a member who has a strong grasp of our message and goes above and beyond to share it with the outside communities, bringing those people into our community...well, that deserves some recognition, don't you think?"

Monica nods her head. "It's not a competition, but we give credit when credit is due."

"That's right, and credit is most certainly due here. Emily, you've been a force of nature ever since you first stepped into the building. I'm so impressed by everything you've accomplished in the short amount of time you've been with us, and I'm excited to see what's to come. I know we don't usually do these one-off ribbon ceremonies, but we decided to make a special exception for you based on your performance at Facebook this afternoon."

Still swelling with a combination of nervousness and sheer elation, Emily smooths the fabric at the sides of her skirt to help come down and regain a semblance of calm. She clears her throat. "Thank you so much," Emily says, pausing to take a deep belly breath in and out. "Not just for this celebration, but for taking a chance on me and for allowing me to flourish here. As some of you might know, I was in a bad place before I joined Fiducia. When Monica found me, I was strung out and desperate. I didn't care about my life, and I didn't have a future that meant anything to me. But because she believed in me, and taught me how to believe in myself, I was able to make a positive change and start fresh. I'm not sure where I would be if she hadn't taken me under her wing that day."

Everyone in the room starts cheering and clapping.

Monica puts her arm over Emily and gives her a hug from the side. "You're getting the Salesforce account," Monica whispers into Emily's ear. A jittery warmth washes over Emily, and she lets out a small yelp of excitement, surprising herself. She looks over at Casey who is frowning and looking down at his phone. He notices Emily looking at him and puts the phone back in his pocket.

Casey lifts his hands to signal for everyone to stop clapping.

"Shall we have some cake now?" Casey asks.

*****

The next day Emily arrives at HQ early in the morning and takes the elevator down to the basement. Aside from a few panels of fluorescent lighting, the hallway is dark and feels unfriendly. When she was in high school, she would eat her lunch with Becca in an empty hallway like this. Sometimes other kids joined in, but it was mostly just the two of them. Emily would share her lunch with Becca, usually some soup or stew in a thermos like the deliciously sour Sinigang na Baboy or a hearty Pinakbet, alongside a small metal box containing a cold noodle salad.

Becca was always grateful for those meals, and Emily cherished her companion's presence. Since she was the first daughter, Emily was in charge at home. This freed her mother to focus her energy on Xiào Lì. The responsibility of taking care of Michael, cleaning the house, making lunches, and preparing dinner after school all fell on Emily, on top of the school work she took home each day. The familial chores were a large load for her to manage, but she always had it under control. Becca's older sister had the same role as Emily in her family, but Becca's sister wasn't much of a cook. The brown bagged lunches Becca brought from home were a scattered assortment of grab-and-go items like yogurt and Little Debbie Swiss Rolls. Sometimes the girls ate the junk food for dessert, and other times they bartered the items during class to get quarters to play arcade games on Sundays after church.

Approaching Casey's office, Emily pushes back her reminiscences and smooths her long tresses from scalp to tip. Emily hadn't called ahead or planned a meeting with Casey but didn't think it would be too much of an imposition to pop into this office and thank him again for taking a chance on her. Since working with Fiducia, she's come to realize that not every new recruit has gotten the kind of treatment and encouragement that she received upon joining. The fact that Monica, a top-ranking Sodalis, basically Casey's second in command, had taken her under her wing is a fact that did not go unnoticed by Emily. Like Becca and those home-cooked bagged lunches, Emily was extremely appreciative of the attention being paid to her.

The door to Casey's office is partially ajar, and Emily knocks lightly then walks in. The room is painted white and unadorned, aside from the massive black filing cabinets lining the walls. Cheri's desk is to the left of the door, and an area toward the back of the room with a hammock hanging from the ceiling is where Emily heard Casey spends most of his time when he's at HQ and not making his rounds. Despite Casey's prominence in the organization, the office is quite small. One would think that Fiducia's founder and CEO would want an extravagant and richly decorated workspace to match his title. Perhaps the austere aesthetic in comparison to the rest of the building is a nod to the humble nature of Fiducia's purpose.

Seeing that the office is unattended, Emily turns to exit but stops when she hears a muffled moaning sound. "Hello? Is someone there?" Emily asks, scanning the floors, trying to find where the sound is coming from. Looking behind Cheri's desk, Emily sees a huddled form and gasps.

"Mindy?" Emily says. She leans over and touches the young woman's shoulder. "Are you okay?"

Mindy opens her eyes wide as if jolted from death. Her eyebrows raise. "Where am I?" she asks.

"You're in Cipher's office. Did you get lost?"

"What time is it?" Mindy asks, rubbing her forehead.

Emily looks at her watch. "It's 5 a.m. Did you hit your head? You don't look well."

"My brain feels like it's pounding."

"Let's get you up. I'll call us a Lyft to Saint Francis Memorial, it's not too far from here."

Emily helps Mindy to her feet and puts her arm around her. "Just lean on me and we'll head over to the elevator."

"Thank you for helping me, but I don't want to get you in trouble."

"It's no trouble. My work can wait. I just want to make sure you don't have a concussion."

The two walk slowly to the elevator. Mindy moans and Emily wonders what happened to her and why she ended up in Casey's office. It wasn't too long ago that Emily was spun out of control, making a fool of herself in front of family and coworkers. She was lucky not to have hurt herself accidentally during that time. Lucky that she lived and didn't hurt anyone else all those times she got behind the wheel of her car after having too much to drink. At the elevator, Emily pushes the up button and squeezes Mindy's shoulder, gently. "I need to get my phone from my locker, but as soon as I do we can go to the hospital."

The elevator doors open and before they can step in Cheri rushes out with her arms flapping like a banshee. "Oh Mindy, there you are! I've been looking all over for you!"

"I'm taking her to Saint Francis," Emily says, using half her body to block Cheri from grabbing onto Mindy and the other half to keep the elevator doors open. "I'm worried she might have a concussion."

"A concussion? Oh no, that's not right. Let me take it from here," Cheri says.

"She has no memory of how she got here," Emily says, backing away from Cheri into the elevator with Mindy. "I think she needs to be looked at. I can handle it."

"Cipher just called me, and he needs you in the library,"

Cheri says, following the two women into the elevator. "There are new courses you need to complete before you get started at Salesforce."

"But I—"

"You poor dear," Cheri says to Mindy, cutting Emily off. "I appreciate your help Emily, but this is not your domain. I'll take care of her."

Mindy is staring down at her shoes. Cheri presses the door open button and takes Mindy by the waist back to the office.

"What just happened?" Emily says out loud as the doors close again.

***

A few months have passed since the green ribbon ceremony. It's a Friday morning, just before sunrise, and Emily is lying in bed using the spare moment to meditate and mentally organize her day before getting up and beginning her routine. It would be another ordinary day of studying materials, meeting with clients for one-on-ones, prepping some coursework for her intensive at Salesforce the following week, and finishing her speech for the conference the next day, but her brother threw her a curveball in the form of a text message the day before and now she has to regroup and strategize what to do next.

When was the last time she had spoken to Michael? It must have been at least six months, and that was just a quick back-and-forth asking her if she had ever listened to The Gateway podcast. She told him that she never heard of it but would check it out. That's as far as the conversation went, and she hadn't bothered to investigate the podcast. Who has time to listen to a podcast, anyway? Maybe Michael does when he's stacking boxes or sweeping floors at Xiào Lì.

The text from Michael last night was to let Emily know that he's driving up to San Francisco this weekend to attend an Infected Mushroom concert and wants to crash at her place for a couple nights. Emily saw the text when she woke up around 2 a.m. to check her agenda. She was surprised to see a text from Micheal, and once she read it, little trickles of unresolved trauma started bubbling up in her stomach. So now, before showering and stretching and eating a quick bowl of instant oatmeal, she's pausing and thinking about how to respond.

"Just answer the text, Emily," she says out loud to herself. She picks up the phone and types, *Sure, let's meet at Yamo for dinner tonight. 7 p.m.*

"See? That wasn't so hard," Emily says, rolling her eyes at how much of a dork she can be.

***

After stopping for coffee and having a quick session with one of her clients, Emily arrives at HQ and digs around in her purse for her keycard to open the front door. As she's pulling it out, a man in a gray blazer steps out from behind her and says, "Hey, can I talk to you for a minute?"

Having lived in San Francisco for as long as she has, Emily has grown accustomed to random strangers stopping her and asking her for money. If she has a dollar or some change on her, she'll always give it out when this happens. Her mind is elsewhere. She had just been mentally preparing a list of everything she'll need to do before Michael arrives, as well as topics she wants to cover for the conference she's leading this weekend. She digs through her bag again and says "Sure," handing the man a dollar.

The man looks at the rumpled bill in Emily's hand and waves it off. "I'm from the San Francisco Police Department. I see you've got your keycard. Are you new to Fiducia?"

"Why are you asking?"

"I just want to ask you a few questions about your boss. Do you have some time to chat with me really quick? We can go sit and have a coffee at the Starbucks a block away if you're worried about the others seeing you with me."

"I've already had enough coffee today. What is this about?" Emily asks. She's sticking her chest out and leaning toward the man. "Let me see your badge."

The man sighs and pulls a San Francisco Police Department Detective's badge from his jacket pocket and presents it to Emily. "I'm Detective Willoughby. I've been watching Casey for years. Not officially. But I am building a fraud case against him."

"If you have proof you can prosecute, but I don't have anything to say to you," Emily says, and swipes her keycard. "I have a conference to get ready for, if you'll please excuse me. You're welcome to attend if you'd like. It's at the Fairmont and it's open to the public." She pushes past him and clicks her way to the elevator. A little smile creeps onto her face. She doesn't know where that energy came from, but she feels proud of herself for standing up to a negative person and not letting him try to bring her down. She could use more of whatever that was to help her get through the weekend.

***

Emily and Michael sit side by side at the counter of Yamo, a hole-in-the-wall Burmese restaurant not far from Emily's apartment. Hungry diners stand outside waiting for a seat at the tiny cash-only establishment. Pots and pans clang and bubble on the hot stove tops behind the counter as the chef busily prepares meals for the many customers.

"You know, they're worried about you," Michael says in a flat tone before shoving an entire samusa into his mouth. "Māma especially."

"She's always worried. She should be happy I'm out of her house," Emily says, twirling her chopsticks into her plate of garlic noodles.

"It's annoying how much she talks about you, when I'm the one who stuck around."

"What do you mean? You've always been her favorite. I couldn't have gotten away with half the stunts you managed to pull," Emily says, pausing to slurp some noodles. "Remember when you had that party?"

"Yeah, she went easy on me, but it's only because she didn't think I'd amount to much. You were the star. All her hopes were riding on you."

"The only times I've ever seen her really smile were when you were telling her some fantastic story you'd make up just for her. Like you'd see a pretty bird branched on a tree but then turn the experience into a full-on love sonnet to the sky."

Michael laughs, then scratches his head. "Did I really used to do that?"

Emily chuckles. "Yeah. All the time."

"Curry chicken," the worker behind the counter says, handing over a plate to Michael.

"This looks amazing," Michael says.

"Everything they make here is superb. And it's cheap, too," Emily says.

"Aren't you making the big bucks now?" Michael asks.

Ever since Emily moved up to San Francisco she hasn't had to think about money or budgeting. Everything is taken care of. Fiducia pays her rent and health insurance and pays a commission for every new recruit she brings in. The bonus she received when she took on Salesforce as her corporate client was very generous as well, though the balance is escrowed through Fiducia. Once a week, Cheri hands Emily an envelope of cash, her weekly allowance, that she uses for things like buying coffee in the morning and occasional clothes shopping trips at Westfield Mall.

"I mean, I'm not hurting for cash. How's the business going back home?" Emily asks, changing the topic.

"You know, not great. I'm glad I can help them, but I can't wait to do something else."

"What are you doing to make that happen?"

Michael takes a bite of his curry chicken and chews, looking down at his plate. "I'm not like you. I can't just leave them hanging," he says. Awkward to begin with, the mood between the brother and sister has taken a frosty turn.

"That's not fair," Emily says. "If I hadn't left, I don't know if I'd still be here. Fiducia saved my life."

"Yeah," Michael says, still looking down.

"Listen, I'm sorry I left the way that I did. That wasn't fair to you, and I recognize that."

"They're always talking about you, you know. You should really call them sometime. I think Māma is worried."

"She's always worried. Maybe if you tell her how great I'm doing up here she'll lighten up a bit," Emily says, finishing the last of her noodles.

"Do you think you can come to the concert tonight? I have an extra ticket," Michael says.

Emily puts some cash down on the counter and stands so the person waiting in line at the door can take a seat. Michael takes his last bite and stands to leave with Emily.

"I should head home. I have a ton of work I need to do,"

she says, slipping into her jean jacket.

"On a Friday night?" Michael asks.

"There's always something to do," Emily says. "Plus, this weekend we have a big conference that I'm leading since Cipher and the Sodales are out of town doing some evangelism in Colorado. You should come and check it out, I think it would be good for you."

"What do I have to do?"

"You don't have to do anything. Just show up. Here," Emily says, handing Michael a key. "This is for my apartment. I'll probably still be up whenever you get back, but just in case."

"You sure you can't come? Even just a couple hours?" Michael asks.

"I really shouldn't," Emily says.

"C'mon, Em. I came all the way up here to see you. Don't you still have some of that wild spirit in you?"

Emily scrunches up her nose like she's trying to hold a sneeze in. She lets out a deep breath and says, "Okay, but just a couple hours."

***

"So, you're sober now, huh?" Michael says, taking a swig of the draft beer in a plastic cup from the concession stand. "That's good."

Emily nods. The concert hall with all the soundchecks and the increasingly drunken patrons is not the best place to have a deep conversation, but Emily appreciates that Mike is reaching out in a show of forgiveness. It's hard to believe her meltdown was less than a year ago. It feels like so much time has passed and so much has changed since then for the better.

"I mean, it's not like I was ever a big drinker. I was being self-destructive in the easiest seeming way. I thought I deserved it."

Michael wraps his arm around Emily's shoulders. "You're my big sister and I'll always look up to you. Except when you're doing stupid stuff."

"Wow, thanks, Mike," Emily says, laughing. "You know I look up to you, too. I wish I had your patience when it comes to our parents."

Mike shakes his head. "Bàba did something kind of crazy a couple weeks ago."

"Crazy how?"

"Māma made dinner and asked me to bring him down to the table, but he wasn't in his room or anywhere else in the house. I looked out the window in the yard and couldn't find him, but then I went out there into the garden and found him curled up beside his tomato plants."

"He was napping?"

"Yeah, just chillin'. With the tomatoes."

"Why was he out there? Is he okay?"

"Yeah, he was fine. I woke him up and he looked surprised, but he told me he just felt sleepy and got comfortable out there."

"That's really weird. I should call him."

"You should call him anyway. I think he really was hurt by the way that you left. He hasn't been the same."

***

The next morning Emily gently nudges her brother, fast asleep on the couch in the living room. He farts and rolls over.

"Mike," she says, just above a whisper.

Michael rolls over again and opens his eyes. "What time is it?" he asks.

"It's 5:30. I need to head over to HQ and grab some things before going to the Fairmont."

Michael sits up on the couch and scratches his head. His sleepy eyes make him look like a little boy who's just been woken from his nap. Cute and cranky, just like Emily remembered from when they were kids.

"I'll come with you. Just let me get dressed," Michael says, standing up and scrambling with his stuff strewn about on the floor.

"Okay, but you'll have to wait in the lobby. Only members are allowed in the building."

"So, what, you can't give me a tour?"

"I can give you a tour of the lobby," Emily says.

"Okay, whatever," Michael says.

Emily waits in the vestibule while Michael finishes getting dressed and cleaned up. Together they make the short trek from Emily's apartment to the MUNI stop down the hill.

"So is every weekend like this?" Michael asks, as the train pulls up to the stop.

"Pretty much," Emily says. "There's always something to prepare for, materials to read, seminars to attend."

"And how much are they paying you, for all this time you spend? Does everyone at Fiducia do this much?"

Emily feels defensive, but this isn't the first time someone has questioned her choice to dedicate so much of her life to spreading Fiducia's gospel. Outsiders, those who have already made up their minds about what the organization is all about, are always quick to judge. She's converted quite a few naysayers, though. It just takes the right amount of persuasion and questioning of the other party's prejudices to get them to her side.

"It's not about the money, Michael. What if I told you that people are living better lives because of what I do? Are they overcoming their fears and taking control of their environments to maximize the potential they already possess? My job is to help people realize that they already have the answers, they just need to figure out how to decode them."

"And are you really doing that?"

"Just last week, one of the first clients I took on told me that she finished her screenplay and found an agent who's now shopping it to major movie studios. When we first met, she was stuck in a bad writer's block. She hadn't written more than a few paragraphs in years."

"So, you sold her a class and she was able to write again?"

"It's not that simple. We worked together for weeks trying to pinpoint what was holding her back. Once she located the source, I was able to guide her out of the rut she had built around herself. She had that screenplay within herself the entire time, she just needed help externalizing it."

"I feel like you're selling me something."

"Just because you're getting an online psychology degree doesn't mean you know everything. If you can try to keep an open mind, I think you'll be pleasantly surprised today. And maybe you'll even be able to unlock some unused potential within yourself."

"It just sounds like a cult. They want all your time and attention. It's another wall you've built around yourself."

"It's not like that. It really isn't."

"We'll see."

***

Emily is sitting on her favorite bench at Dolores Park wrapping up a session with a client when she feels her phone buzzing in her bag. It buzzes again a moment later, and then her ringer goes off indicating that someone, likely whoever just texted her multiple times, is now calling her.

"Do you need to take that?" her client asks.

Emily pulls out her phone. Cheri's calling.

"I'll call them back. Let's just focus on you," Emily says, turning the ringer off and putting the phone back in her bag.

By the end of the session, Emily is frazzled and decides to stop for a pick-me-up cup of coffee before heading back to HQ. It's been two days since Michael went back to Aliso Viejo and she's still paddling through the emotions he stirred up. His visit was unexpected and didn't go the way she had wanted. He seemed happy to see her at first, like he almost forgot about her grief meltdown. He was the same old Mike, teasing and cracking jokes, but it seemed like he was holding something back.

When she tried to get him to open up to her, he just threw it back in her face, as if she hadn't been making tremendous strides to improve herself. And when she called on him to join her on stage at the Fairmont for a hot seat interview, he averted his eyes and walked out of the conference. Left her looking stupid on stage holding a microphone out to no one.

Outside the coffee shop with a fresh latte, Emily pulls out her phone again and reads the five new text messages from Cheri, back in town with Casey and the Sodales after the Colorado trip and doing damage control.

Meet me ASAP after your session. I'm at the cafe at Union Square.

Was that your brother at the conference? We all watched the recording, and we were not pleased.

You know you're not supposed to associate with negative people.

Casey asked me to talk to you about it. We don't want any further negative associations around Fiducia.

It's one thing to convert nonbelievers in a closed setting but it's a very bad look to cause a scene like that during one of our open sessions.

Emily lets out a long sigh. Ever since that day when she found Mindy in the basement with a banged up head, she's tried to steer clear of Cheri. Whatever happened in Casey's office that day had been kept quiet. Even Monica, who seemed to know everything that happened behind closed doors at Fiducia, didn't have an answer. When Emily asked her, Monica looked confused then shook her head. It was as if the events of that morning were stricken from the record.

A tangled mass of anxiety starts coiling out within Emily's belly as she makes the short trek to Union Square to meet Cheri.

I'll be there in a few minutes. Just wrapped my session, Emily texts back.

Cheri is sitting alone at a table, legs crossed, back straight, on the East side of Union Square. Her phone is out and she's busy texting or emailing someone when Emily makes her way over.

"Thanks for meeting with me," Emily says, and sits down. Cheri rolls her eyes only slightly.

"You know this is bad for you, right? We trusted you with this conference and you really screwed us." Cheri says, putting her phone down in front of her on the table.

Emily leans forward. "It won't happen again."

"It better not. We don't want to take Salesforce away from you, but we will if you fuck up again. You're supposed to be a good judge of character, and you're supposed to predict what people will do when you speak to them."

"Last weekend was the first time I had seen or talked to my brother since coming here, and he just didn't understand how much I'm helping people. I thought I could show him, but he is too stubborn. He thinks he knows everything."

"You have to cut him off," Cheri says. Her face is blank, and her eye contact is flesh-piercing.

Emily stares back. "I already have."

***

The next day, Emily is sitting in the cafeteria at HQ eating another one of Chef's vegetarian creations, a lasagna of sorts made with eggplant pounded thin and fried in between layers of cashew cheese and a spicy tomato sauce. It's delicious and filling and Emily eats it slowly and carefully while reading her latest coursework.

She looks up and sees Casey step off the elevator with Cheri trailing behind him holding a stack of three-ring binders, the type of binders Casey uses for storing his charts and essays before they get typed up and printed into booklets. They stop at a coffee table near the windows and plop down on the floor pillows to sit face to face. Cheri takes notes as Casey speaks.

Emily refocuses her attention on the worksheets before her but soon starts daydreaming. It's been less than a week since Michael's visit, but he's texted her twice, urging her to come back home. Bring her back into the grip of negativity. He just couldn't see how much things had changed for the better. Maybe he couldn't stand to see Emily living the life she had always wanted, no longer under their mother's thumb.

And hasn't her life improved? Didn't she discover meaning in improving the lives of others? Once she joined, her time and energy funneled into Fiducia, bringing her all and dedicating her life to the cause. Always showing up and staying present. Not a moment to stop and question anything. Concerning herself with the needs of her mentors and her trainees. She wants to believe she is helping to save the world, but is she actually? And is she neglecting real life in this pursuit of a higher purpose?

When was the last time she had thought about Becca? Becca, oh, Becca. Beloved Becca. Her face floats in Emily's mind's eye, faded and pixelated like a degraded digital photo. Everything is distorted, the shape of her mouth isn't quite right, her eyes like miniature black holes swirling and sucking her back into her past. What would Becca say if she could see what Emily's been up to? Would she approve? Would she be happy for her? Emily isn't sure if she can still remember what Becca's voice sounded like.

Monica's voice booms from the other end of the cafeteria, snapping Emily back to reality.

"It's all gone, Cipher. Where did it go?" Monica stands over Casey, still seated at the coffee table looking absolutely lackadaisical, leaning backward with one arm behind him.

"I don't know what you're talking about." He blinks slowly, then grins. Cheri stands up as if to shield Casey from the forcefulness of Monica's voice.

"You know exactly what I'm talking about. I just got off the phone with my financial planner and my entire nest egg is gone."

This little scene has attracted the attention of the dozen or so members who were previously minding their own business eating eggplant lasagna. All eyes in the room are watching Monica and Casey.

"I'm certain that you are mistaken, Monica. Seems like you were sold a bill of goods and you're looking for someone to blame when you should be blaming yourself. And if I were you, I would watch how you're speaking to me right now."

Monica lowers her voice to a hiss. "I know it was you. Don't you ever forget that I know you. And I know how to bury you. Casey."

"Why don't you go home and rest?" Casey says. His tone remains flat and calm. "You're not getting enough sleep and it's making you hysterical. Cheri, can you please walk Monica out?"

Cheri takes Monica by the arm and starts walking her

toward the elevator, but Monica jerks away, shaking herself loose. "I'll see myself out," she says then saunters toward the stairwell, opening the door causing the alarm to sound. Emily flinches. Several members put their hands over their ears. Everyone seems shocked to hear the blaring siren that no one before ever dared to trigger.

Casey grabs Cheri by the waist. "After you turn off the alarm, I need you to type up a memo. Get it widespread ASAP."

Cheri smiles down on Casey. "Yes, Cipher."

Emily is stunned. What on earth did she just witness? Is Monica okay?

Why didn't I run over there to protect her? she wonders.

Casey looks around the room and once the members realize he's aware that they've been watching him, they all resume their mundane tasks and eat their meals.

Once the alarm silences, Emily waits for what she considers a safe amount of time and then heads for the elevator, trying to make herself as inconspicuous as possible. At her locker, she checks her phone to see if any new appointments were added to her calendar for the day and sees an email that Fiducia HQ sent just moments ago. It's labeled "important." Emily opens it and almost chokes on her own saliva when she reads the headline: "CHILD KILLER: MONICA SAMUELS," followed by a photo of Monica with her eyes crossed out.

"What is this?" Emily says out loud to herself. Her

fingers tremble as she calls Monica, but it goes straight to voicemail.

Without thinking, Emily grabs her things and takes the elevator down to the lobby. When she gets outside, she runs. Her pace is frantic as she races down Sutter Street, cutting through crowds of shoppers and office workers on their lunch break, then up the hill to Pine Street.

Just call a Lyft she thinks to herself, pausing to catch a breath at a red light. She pulls her phone out.

***

The air is colder and fresher in Seacliff. With a view of the ocean and the Golden Gate Bridge, the historic and stately two-story brick mansion where Monica lives is easily worth five million dollars. Emily looks up at the building from the sidewalk, in admiration and with some trepidation. Is Monica home now? She breathes in deeply and pushes the fearful feeling out with an exhale.

***

"You know this thing withstood the 1906 earthquake?" Monica had told Emily the first time she visited for afternoon tea. "Not too many places in this area can say the same."

"Your home is beautiful," Emily had said. "It seems so

peaceful here."

"It's a great place to unwind, though I'm hardly ever here," Monica had said.

***

Before ringing the doorbell, Emily tries Monica's cell again. Straight to voicemail.

Emily grabs the large brass knocker, shaped like a wolf's head carrying a heavy ring in its mouth. Lifting the ring, she knocks three times and waits. Nothing. Then, Emily remembers the back entrance. Around the back, up the private drive and through a garden gate, Emily crosses a wild yard of boulders, overgrown succulents, and other native flora. The kitchen window is slightly open. Emily grabs an Adirondack chair to stand on and forces the window open more. She hoists herself up and slips inside.

"Monica? Are you here? Monica?" she calls out, her voice softly echoing against the minimalist decor, then creeps up the stairs to the bedroom.

The door is shut but unlocked. Emily knocks, then opens the door to see Monica lying on the floor next to her bed. Open prescription bottles litter her bedside table.

"Oh my god, Monica!" she shouts, and props Monica's limp body up against the bed. Struggling with her phone's fingerprint lock, she calls 911.

"Is she breathing?" the emergency operator asks.

"I think so, but it feels weak," Emily says.

"I'm going to need you to lay her on her back and start doing chest compressions, now just follow my lead," the emergency operator says.

"Can you get someone here now? It looks like she took a bunch of different pills."

"We have an ambulance on the way, but until they get to you, I need you to listen to me. Do you understand?"

"Yes," Emily says.

"Okay, now center both your hands on her chest with your shoulders directly above your arms. I'm going to count to 30 and with every count you need to press down hard. Ready? 1, 2, 3, 4, 5, 6..."

Time moves slowly and quickly simultaneously, blurring everything around her and drowning out all sound. No thoughts pass through her head. Emily is at once present and non-existent. All she knows is that she is trying to save her friend's life using her full body weight to the rhythm of a voice over speakerphone. When the doorbell rings, she is jolted back to sentience.

"Someone's at the door," she says out loud.

"That's the ambulance, go and answer the door," the emergency operator says.

Emily jumps up and rushes down the stairs and swings the front door open with such force she feels as if she could tear it from the frame.

"She's upstairs," she says to the EMTs. "Hurry."

***

Disinfectant hangs heavy in the air and stings Emily's nostrils as she shuffles down the hallway at the hospital from the waiting area to the room where Monica has just woken up. Emily's skirt is rumpled from the activity of the evening, including the several hours spent intermittently pacing the sidewalk outside the ER and trying to make herself comfortable in the cloddish wooden seating provided for expectant loved ones.

"She's still a bit groggy, but you can go in to see her if you'd like," a nurse had said.

From the doorway she sees Monica lying on her side facing the window overlooking the parking lot. Emily knocks on the open door softly.

"Hey, they told me you woke up," Emily says.

"Oh, Emily," Monica sighs, rolling over slowly.

Emily steps toward the bed and reaches out for Monica's hand. "How are you feeling?"

Monica closes her eyes. Hot tears roll down her face. "My life is ruined."

"Do you want to talk about it?" Emily asks. Gentle, quiet, the way she would want to be approached, how she wished she had been approached after Becca, when she needed it the most. "I'm here for you. I want to help."

A look of stilted terror washes over Monica's face. Her eyes are wide and glassy, staring at the wall and staring through it, some fictional distance to a memory reanimating and turning into words. "There's so much I could tell you. You'll think I'm crazy."

"I don't think you're crazy. You're the most solid person I know."

"I trust you," Monica says, looking into Emily's eyes. "And I'm sorry for dragging you into this. If I had known what I know now—"

Monica's voice trails off. With great concentration, she swallows hard before taking a deep breath. "I thought I was doing something good. I thought I was helping people. Only in the last few weeks have I started to put together what Casey's been doing with our finances. All of ours. Even my retirement fund I started back when I was at my old job. He's been siphoning funds and doing who knows what the fuck with it."

"Is that why those detectives were at HQ last week?"

"That could be part of it."

"Part of it?"

"There's a lot you don't know about Casey. A lot no one knows about Casey. I was one of the first members of Fiducia. I knew him when we were both in college and was with him through his dark times. I know some things about his past that no one else knows. I know where the skeletons are hidden, literally and figuratively. Consequently, he knows things about me that I've never shared publicly."

"The email—"

"That email was to smear me, discredit me, and make me look unstable. He's got files on everyone. All of our secrets, primed and ready to be used as blackmail against us at a moment's notice."

The moment is interrupted by a loud ringing from Emily's bag.

"Don't answer that," Monica says.

"What?" Emily says, feeling around for the vibrating device and glancing at the screen to see who could be calling at this hour.

"They might be trying to find me."

"It's just my brother. But I don't know why he'd call me in the middle of the night."

"Please don't tell him about what happened."

"I won't," Emily says, answering the call. "Mike?" She can hear him breathing into the phone. "Mike," she repeats. "Are you there?"

"I have some," Michael says, pausing. "Bad news." His voice cracks at the word, "bad."

A cold tickle rushes down Emily's back, and she shivers. "What's going on?"

"Bàba passed away today. We need you to come home."

Part 3

Written by Risha Mae Ordas

Emily Wang is no stranger to grief. She has had it coat her tongue and live in her lungs like it was the air she breathed for life. She cries for what feels like hours with her little brother Michael, and for a moment they transport back in time to when they would cry to each other when they were younger, more naive.

As soon as the void in her heart was filled with the adrenaline rush of leaving San Francisco as fast as she could, Emily drops everything and drives to the airport like a madwoman. No packing, no goodbyes other than making sure Monica is alive and situated. Becca's gone; she couldn't have lost her father too. Not now, not when Monica just got out of the hospital. Not when it seems like her life with Fiducia was built on nothing but smoke and mirrors. Life hasn't been going her way recently, but it was never that unkind up until the time she got home. By the time her plane lands, his viewing room is being prepared. Her father, a strong sensible pillar of the family, died before his eldest daughter was able to come home. She wasn't able to see him alive.

This fact still hits her like a freight train even after three days since she got home. It is a place she no longer recognizes. The once-bright house her parents bought is now filled with empty bottles of chemo pills neatly filed in a corner, a hospital bed fitted in what used to be a living room, and several boxes of different Chinese goods overflowing from Xiào Lì. The misplaced ginseng tea and Chun Guang Coconut Candy that were supposed to be housed in Xiào Lì truly make her feel like the world was off-kilter. It takes a second for her to regain focus now. She's back in her old room.

The first things she sees every morning are the dark gray ceilings she chose during her angsty teenage phase. In this life she is living now, gray ceilings are all wrong. She must wake up to the light lavender ceilings of her Mission apartment. Her pillows feel wrong too—it should be the cheap memory foam pillow from the dollar store. Her blanket is wrong. The way the window cracks when she closes it. The temperature of her room. The way her father is still dead every time she opens her eyes to another new day. Now she truly feels like she has nothing.

Emily is not part of the funeral preparations—Michael took care of all that. Death had been a long time coming for her Bàba, her little brother says. As much as she wanted to be involved, her brother was insistent he had things handled. Of course, Mrs. Wang thinks otherwise.

"Lì, why are you not helping Xiào Lì call up the insurance company? Isn't that something you could do?" She heard her mother complain about it one day.

"I would if he would let me, Māma," Emily complained.

"You ask again," her mother's sharpness cut through the silence of the empty viewing room. It was early afternoon, no one was scheduled to visit her father yet. But it was the last day of the viewing, and traditionally everyone would come in droves once night came. "You know how stubborn that boy is."

"Wonder where he got that from," she whispered, discreetly rolling her eyes.

Emily spies the skies slowly changing color and checks the time on her phone. Her wallpaper is still the old family photo they took when Xiào Lì opened. She changed it the day her Māma called her the last time before her Bàba went on life support.

"Come home," she could hear her mother's voice crackle through the receiver. However, that was the time Monica was having issues at Fiducia.

"I'm sorry, I can't right now. There's a lot of things happening at work," the excuses stumbled clumsily out of her mouth. Emily could sense that Monica wasn't well. Even though that gut feeling turned out to be correct, she didn't know if it was worth staying with her when it meant seeing her mother's devastated face as soon as she arrived at the funeral parlor.

"Sorry, I'm late. My stupid flight got delayed," Emily said as she entered the viewing room.

Mrs. Wang rushed over and immediately hugged her tightly and sobbed. "Where were you, my child? Where were you?"

Emily felt her mother's body shake as she cried against her shoulder. Emily wrapped her arms around her just as tight.

"Your Bàba is gone, Lì. Where were you?" She repeats. Emily didn't know what to answer.

Michael is more standoffish. After greeting Emily at the

funeral parlor, their interactions are limited to exchanging plans about the pasiyam. If she were more honest with herself, she could understand why. After all, it was he who tried to convince her to go back and visit. It was he who called her in the early morning. It was he who took care of their parents when she was off to San Francisco doing God knows what. And now, it's still him who's at the helm of a wayward ship that just lost its captain.

Soft scratching catches her attention. Like clockwork, she rises before the sun gets a chance to coat her room in light. She hears a soft meow at the other side of the door, and she couldn't help the small smile on her face. Her life became unrecognizable in just a day, but Bao is still Bao—something she will be forever grateful for. She opens the door, and the proud ragdoll trots his way in the room and leaps onto her bed. Bao looks at her expectantly, waiting for her to get back on the bed so he can snuggle beside her. Emily can't help the giggle bubbling up. He's turning eight this year and his antics are still that of a spoiled kitten. She lies down and Bao immediately positions himself under her armpit while Emily winds her body around the animal.

"Bao?" she whispers, absentmindedly stroking his fur. The cat purrs. "Am I a bad person?" As if understanding the question, he answers with a soft trill. "Why is this always happening to me?" The cat looks at her, head tilted to the side before offering another meow.

"If I am evil, then is this penance?" She hugs Bao closer. "I didn't go to my best friend's funeral." Tears seal Emily's eyes. "I thought I was doing better, but why does everything feel like it's all my fault?"

Bao offers no more answers, just purrs. She pours her grief into the only warmth since she got here. She allows the suffocating sorrow to shake her body while she ruminates on her broken heart. Emily is fully aware that she does not have the luxury to wallow—not then, not now. Once she feels the pain has momentarily left her body, she picks herself up from the bed and starts to get ready for the day. She's on day duty in the funeral parlor today. She tries her best to put herself together, but she knows she can never shake the haunted lingering in her eyes.

***

The second day of her stay is when Emily buries her father in the dirt. The funeral is a quiet affair for Emily even though the people gathered are relatively large. After her tearful welcome, Emily doesn't hear her mother cry at all, even throughout the sermon or through the eulogy she gave. Emily feels like the lack of weight it usually carries. The fanfare and the dread that she is used to when someone dies was nowhere near her father even at the end.

The pasiyam begins at the Wang house as a get-together of the guests. A much livelier event. The Wang trio is busy preparing lunch for the guests while accepting condolences from many. Some were their neighbors—Schwartz, Niedermeyer, Chen, friends who have been staples around her life in the Wang household. Some other faces Emily cannot recognize. She is proud to see the Asian-American community they have met through Xiào Lì.

"I'm sorry for your loss dear," Mrs. Santiago says when Emily offers the gossiping aunties biko slices from the kitchen. A small hug is exchanged before Mrs. Santiago returns to the conversation with the other aunties who were sniffing out canards they could feast on once the festivities conclude. Emily scans the crowd for her brother and finds him entertaining guests, hopping from one boozy uncle to newer patrons of Xiào Lì.

During Emily's time in Fiducia, she mastered the art of neatly folding her grief like origami. Losing Becca was a huge blanket she was constantly wrapped in, not knowing where it ended and where she began. She didn't know what to do with herself, but Fiducia taught her to transform her loneliness into fragile paper cranes that she would have to address sometime later. But now, she has to mingle with faces that she either has not seen in years or never seen in her lifetime. This was what she was good at, as Monica had pointed out to her.

Emily weaves through the crowd. She reconnects with old childhood playmates, refills platters of dumplings, and passes plates of kakanin when their neighbor arrives with a fresh batch. *It is like I belong back home*, she muses. But in reality, she is just as good at taking other people's grief and folding it into origami, too. Only now, she wonders, if the grief she helped other people fold felt this rotten and heavy.

As she rests with some kakanin, her phone pulses in the pocket of her dress. She puts her plate down to investigate, only for her blood to run cold when she sees her mentor's name. Flashes of worry and relief synonymously mix with guilt as she schools herself to answer the call.

"Monica? Oh my God, are you okay?"

"Em?" Monica answers. "Are you at your house?"

Emily raises a brow. "Yeah. Today was the funeral, of course, I'm home. Why do you ask?"

"Your house is the one with the yellow tulips in the flower box, right?"

"Yes but how do you know that? Where are you?"

"I'm at your porch. Can you come meet me outside?"

Confusion blazes through the meticulous paper cranes of her grief. Her feelings have still not settled. She immediately excuses herself from the kitchen to storm at the front door. Michael already beat her to it. She hears him ask Monica who she is, so Emily quickly cuts in.

"Mike!" Emily calls out, which causes some eyes to peer through the door curiously. "I'll take it from here."

She can feel her brother's weary eyes on her before he shakes his head. "Not today, jiě jie."

She watches him about to tell Monica off, but she places a hand on his arm.

"You sure?"

"Yes."

Emily doesn't return the concerned gaze and instead focusing on the forlorn expression of her friend. "I'll talk to her outside."

Michael closes the door behind Emily as she ushers Monica away from prying eyes.

"How are you now?" Emily asks, her concern bubbling up like clockwork. "Are you okay to travel?"

"Yeah, Em. I'm fine," Monica waves her hand dismissively.

"Good." A beat. "But why are you here? How did you find my house?"

"Okay I know this is creepy showing up at your house like this," Monica replies. "You left your ID out. And as an emergency contact for me—"

Monica is on the verge of tears. Emily can see her mentor look to the side where the pristine tulips are, before turning her gaze back to her.

"Thank you, Em. You didn't have to do that for me."

"I know I didn't," Emily responds. Silence envelops the two women. The chatter of the pasiyam simmers morphs into a chorus of prayers starts to echo from the inside. "Why are you here, Monica?"

"I wanted to say thank you in person, Em. Choosing to stay with me instead of going home must have been so hard."

Emily doesn't know what to expect, but Monica's genuine feelings seem hollow. There are a million questions still swarming in her head that she cannot sort out yet, but she finds herself unable to ask any of them.

"If that is all..." Emily bobs her head in the door's

direction and sighs. "I've got to go back inside." She detects Monica's thoughts going a mile a minute before she speaks.

"I am sorry for your loss. And...for what it's worth, I'm sorry. For everything else."

Emily nods. "Thank you for coming all the way here." She mulls her next words over for a brief second. "Can we not do this here? I don't think I can handle this now."

"I understand. I'm sorry, Em. I didn't mean to hurt you."

"Well, you did."

Monica's face crumples. "I did it for Fiducia. I thought I was doing the right thing."

Before Emily can find an answer, the front door opens. Prayers spilled out of the patio along with Mrs. Wang and her usual stern expression. She eyes her daughter once before assessing her companion.

"Are you new in the neighborhood?" The matriarch asks.

"No, ma'am. I'm sorry to bother you," Monica quickly replies. "I just wanted to offer my condolences to Em and her family. I presume you're Mrs. Wang. Please accept my deepest condolences."

Mrs. Wang nods slowly in response. Emily feels her skin prickle at her mother's gaze. Once she arrived, she was honest to her family about the reason for her staying in San Francisco. At that time, her mother seemed accepting of it. But never did she expect her and Monica to meet this way, let alone at the funeral. She needs to diffuse her anxiety by offering Monica to go inside and rest, but her mother beats her to it.

"Thank you. You've done what you wanted," Mrs. Wang speaks in a low, menacing tone. "Now please get off my property,"

"Māma!" Emily shouts. The prayer briefly pauses inside the house. Michael is in the background trying to chant a rosary mystery louder. "Monica is my co-worker. Please don't speak to her like that."

"This is final, Lì! I do not want her in my house!" Mrs. Wang turns her back on both women. Emily grabs her by the elbow.

"But Māma! Please. She took care of me in San Francisco. I want her to be a part of this too."

"This is for your own good," Mrs. Wang says tersely. She wriggles from Emily's grip to look at an affronted Monica face-to-face. "Please leave before I call the police."

"Em, it's fine. I'll go."

Mrs. Wang reruns inside, but Emily lingers. "I'm sorry she was being rude."

Monica lowers her gaze. "Talk soon, okay? I want to explain myself. I'll be around." She steps off the porch, leaving Emily to collect herself before going back inside to dodge some of the questions that will surely come her way.

***

At 5 p.m., the guests leave the Wangs' house without much fanfare. While her children are busy putting away the platters, Mrs. Wang plans the meals for the days to come. It is customary to hold a prayer novena for the next nine days with snacks to feed the guests. The Wang matriarch sits in peace, touched that the community has decided to join her for the passing of her husband.

Amidst the clangs of cutlery and the scribble of paper, Emily decides it is time to bring Monica up. "Māma," she starts. Mrs. Wang only replies with a hum. "You shouldn't have been rude to Monica," Emily states while wiping one of the dishes. "I didn't get to say goodbye before I left. She was just making sure I was okay."

"I was only trying to protect you, Lì," Mrs. Wang responds dismissively. "That woman was the reason why you weren't here when your Bàba passed away."

Emily winces, "Don't make it like it's her fault. I chose to stay."

"It's good then that you're going to stay with us for a while, so you won't get to see them."

Michael whips his head around, looking like he has to say something, but Emily beats him to it. She arches her eyebrow. "And when did I ever say that?"

Michael finally speaks. "Māma, we're not talking about this today."

"What?" Emily asks, turning to her little brother. "What are we not talking about?"

Michael sighs. "We can talk about it tomorrow, jiě jie.

First thing."

He takes the dishes he was washing and places them near their mother. Emily hears him whispering something in Mandarin, to which her mother angrily whispers her response.

Emily slams the cling wrap she was holding on the countertop. "Stop talking like I'm not here!" Three sets of eyes are now daggers. "What's so important that you can't tell me, huh? Am I not part of this family anymore? Is that why you didn't want me to help with funeral preparations?"

"You want to find out? Fine!" Mrs. Wang throws the dish towel to the floor. She makes her way to the other side of the island, even when Michael half-heartedly tries to pull her aside. He was still talking to her in Mandarin. Emily desperately wishes she could translate their discussion.

"No, Michael! She wants to know, then fine!" Mrs. Wang shrugs off Michael's attempt at soothing her anger. "This family is bankrupt."

Emily's eyebrows shoot upward to her hairline. "What about Xiào Lì? Didn't you take over, Mike?"

Michael shakes his head. "It's been closed for a month. We couldn't afford to pay both the rent and chemo."

Emily always knew Michael as steadfast. He was usually the calmer one between the siblings so hearing the break in his voice makes Emily's heart ache.

"What?" Emily's eyes widen.

Emily witnesses several emotions flit through her brother's face before he answers her. "Ever since Bàba went home for treatment. We couldn't afford a nurse, so Māma and I have been taking shifts to take care of him."

Had she been that deep in Fiducia that she wasn't able to hear about her family's financial situation? Unbeknownst to her internal turmoil, he continues.

"It's gotten so bad that we could barely afford the funeral. Thank God for Bàba's insurance. But as it is, we won't be able to pay the debt we have accrued."

Hot tears sting Emily's eyes. She clenches her jaw for a moment and counts her breath, just like how she would teach her participants to calm themselves in some of the seminars she routinely gave. She imagines her anguish folding into a cerulean paper she neatly folds into another paper crane.

"I didn't let you help at the funeral because we were hoping to borrow some money from you," Michael adds. "I plan to re-open Xiào Lì. To do that we need to pay the rent we owe and get back in business."

All thoughts about anything else vanish. A wave of molten anger fills Emily's veins and she clenches hard on her fists. "That's it? That's why you want me to stay here? Not because you want me here?"

"It's not like that—" Michael tries to rebut.

"If money is all you need, why do I have to stay?"

Mrs. Wang points a finger at Emily with such a magnetic force, it forces Emily to quiet and listen. "It's time you give back to your family. How are we supposed to eat if the store isn't making money yet?"

"Then borrow money from someone else!"

"You weren't there when Michael and I were taking care of Bàba! This is the least you can do."

"The least *I* can do?" Emily says, enraged. "If you had told me that Bàba was that sick, then I would have come home immediately!"

"Would you? You didn't even believe your brother when he tried to call you home."

Emily becomes a vacuum under pressure. The feeling of shame rises with anger, mixing in a chasm inside her that she wants to bury deep down. "This still doesn't mean you can treat me like your ATM. I'm fucking done with this conversation."

Emily drops everything and vanishes through the back door. She hears her mother's voice fade in the distance, but she tunes everything out in the world. Walking will help, should help. At least that's what Emily tells herself.

✳✳✳

On her third morning in Aliso Viejo, her childhood home is suffocating to live in. The night before, Emily returned to dinner like a filial child but was met with silence. Emily noted two things: that she and Michael talk here and there about topics that are neither here nor there, and that he and her mother have made a routine. They live a life without her which makes her feel out of place more than ever.

Despite this, Emily feels like she can't leave her family with tensions as high as this. There is an obligation that falls on her shoulders, financially and emotionally, for being her mother's firstborn. Something in her scalds at the thought. This was ingrained in her since she was a child, something she and Becca bonded over as firstborn daughters. She used to despise the responsibility of being one. It was so easy when she shared the burden with Becca. But Becca is gone, and her responsibility is now more than just cooking food for Michael and cleaning the house when her parents are at Xiào Lì. How she feels about that, she has yet to decide.

A soft scratch at the door alerts her to her early morning guest. She hoists herself from her bed and opens the door to the fluffy ragdoll, who wraps his tail around her ankles as thanks.

"Good morning to you too, Bao."

At least Bao is someone in the house who did not treat her differently. He confidently snuggles up to her as if he owned the place and Emily was happy to go along with his antics. When she feels no more movement in the house, she sets off for her morning walk. It is her routine in San Francisco and more than ever she wants some semblance of a life she can recognize. She sets sight on the small dog park in their neighborhood when a shrill ringtone disrupts her autopilot actions. She sighs when reading the caller ID.

"Monica, listen," Emily says. "Sorry, but I'm not in the mood right now."

"Well, we can meet at lunch if you'd prefer."

"Mon, I'm serious," Emily persists. "I don't want to hear any more excuses."

There is a beat of silence on the other line and Emily wishes to hang up when a whisper catches her off guard. "I'd like to tell you the truth, please."

Emily closes her eyes. She pretends to think about it, but she knows she's already made up her mind. "Fine. I'll meet you in 30 minutes."

Monica's motives have ached at the back of Emily's head. A low thrum on top of the grief she continues to neatly fold in her head over and over again. She plans to continue to do so, but she also knows Monica will not drop this.

To Emily, it feels anticlimactic to meet at a local Panera Bread to talk. The banality of this fast-food chain isn't befitting whatever truth Monica wanted to tell her, but this was the nearest rendezvous point. Monica is already there, still looking very kept despite being in casual clothes. Monica waves Emily to her table. This was one of the first lessons that she taught her: to use her appearance both as armor and a weapon of persuasion when talking to the people they were supposed to help. Why would anyone trust them if they didn't look the part? After all, Emily used to believe they were changing lives, and she ate that advice up like it was sustenance to keep her alive. Now, she doesn't know if she can take Monica's lessons seriously anymore.

"Hey," Monica greets as soon as she sits down.

"So, what is this truth?" Emily says.

"First off, I want to apologize," Monica says. "I didn't

mean to hurt you."

"That doesn't mean shit, Mon."

Monica's face flushes. "I know. I can't apologize enough. I thought I was doing the right thing."

Emily feels the sizzle of betrayal sear her bones before she can register it. She is instantly reminded of her mother, who is so adept at using her own emotions as battering rams to anyone just to get her way. Emily never feels like there is even a second of her mother caring enough about either her or her brother's feelings. She has always been selfish that way. She thinks herself a fool for thinking Monica was any different.

"What *was* best for me, Monica? We were together almost every day at Fiducia," Emily hisses, trying her best to control her anger. "You could have told me anytime that we were together. I thought I was your friend!"

"And you still are, Em!"

"Then why did I find out while the whole of Fiducia did? Huh? Why did you have to keep lying to me?"

Instantly, Monica's fight in her eye crumples to a sorrow that Emily had only seen once in her life. She was looking at her reflection the night after Becca's funeral.

"Because..." Monica hesitates, before releasing a breath to steady herself. "It was my Alicia who died."

Emily stills. "Who is Alicia?"

"My daughter. She was stillborn," Monica whispers. "I didn't know what else to do in my life before Fiducia." She shoots a pleading gaze at Emily. "Casey gave me a purpose.

I wanted to help others who were as lost as I was."

Emily has a front-row seat to her friend's unraveling. She witnesses the weight on Monica's shoulders as she slumps down and cries. Emily thought that she saw her friend's rock bottom when she was rushed to the hospital. Sitting here in Panera Bread in the middle of the morning seems ill-fitting for Monica and her persona. There are still things they need to talk about, but at this moment, Emily does what she thinks is best. She slides out of her booth and asks Monica to scoot over. Emily goes in for a hug. The pair adjust their sitting positions until Monica is sobbing on her shoulders. A warm hug, something Emily's Bàba did when he was alive, is the only thing that brought her comfort— something she hopes Monica will feel as well.

After the pair leaves Panera, Emily asks Monica to accompany her to their local Costco to pick up more supplies for the pasiyam. The eldest Wang isn't religious by any means, so she wants to use baking pan de sal for the guests as an excuse to not participate in the novena her devout mother was leading.

"Is this the brand of flour you wanted?" Monica asks, pointing to a box of flour on the shelf.

Emily swerves her head to spot what her friend is pointing at. "Yes, two of those, please."

"What's all this for anyway?"

Emily hums, ticking off some of the things they picked up from the list. "It's tradition, I guess. Māma and Michael wanted to do it. They said it was something to help Bàba's soul cross to the other side. Something like that."

A pensive look flits across her mentor's face. "Would it be too late to hold one if the person's long dead?"

Emily reaches for Monica's hand. "It's not," she says. "I think Alicia would like that too."

Monica forces her wobbly lips into a small smile. She frees her hand from Emily and wipes any wayward tears threatening to fall. "Let's do one for her when we get back."

While ticking off each supply on Emily's list, the two women continued sharing about each other's lives before they met. The Costco's aisles serve as a confessional for the two women. Their fellow shoppers fade into the background as Monica tells story after story like rushing water that broke free from a dam.

"I was about to get kicked out, you know."

Emily gasps and drops the packets of yeast. A loud guffaw erupts from her enigmatic mentor which colors her cheeks a little in embarrassment. Adjacent shoppers gaze at the silly antics and soon move on.

"Jesus, it's been a while since I got that reaction. Sorry for laughing, Em."

"It's okay," Emily replies, feeling bashful as she puts the yeast in the cart. "Was this when you were still pregnant?"

"Yes. My parents weren't exactly thrilled that I was pregnant out of wedlock. I tried to convince them that I would be a good parent and get a job. But not long after that I miscarried. They allowed me to stay home after that."

At this, Emily immediately stops pushing the cart and

gives a side hug to Monica, which her mentor graciously accepts.

After clearing the list and getting a few things for Monica's hotel room, the two women soon find themselves in line for the self-checkout. It was here where a familiar figure manages to snag itself on Emily's peripheral vision. Before she could voice anything out, Monica beat her to the punch.

"Is that...Martin Davis?"

Emily permits herself to stare at the man. "Yeah, I think it is." The man surveys the women in a devious manner, then quickly exits the store.

"That's the man who quit gambling, right?" She asks Monica, who hastily scans her grocery items. "Didn't he get promoted to team leader last month?"

"Well, what the fuck is he doing in Aliso Viejo?" Monica comments as she hauls a reusable grocery bag on her shoulders. "He's always been creepy, but this is extra."

Emily feels a prickle on the back of her neck and comments absentmindedly, "Yeah."

The pair arrives at Monica's hotel, but the uneasy feeling still hangs between the two women. Emily parks the car nearest to the entrance so her friend would have an easier time gathering groceries. The sky is overcast at midday but some rain pitters onto the windshield. Emily hopes that it will not rain too badly for her father's pasiyam. As Monica gathers the rest of her remaining grocery bags, Emily spots a shady figure staring at the rental car intently.

"What are you looking at, Em?" Monica asks, trying to see what her friend is fixated on. Realization dawns on her, her face contorting in horror. "No way. Isn't that Ezekiel Young? The ex-Mormon?"

Emily nods. "And ex-military."

"Now this is getting out of hand. First Martin, and now Ezekiel?" Monica huffs. "Thank God for tinted windows, am I right?"

"You don't think they're following us, do you?" Emily whispers.

Monica clenches her grocery bags. "Only one way to find out!"

"Wait, no!"

Monica opens the door before Emily can finish her protest. Some groceries spill out, but she pays no mind. She looks to Emily who regards her with anxious exasperation.

"Sorry Em," she mutters. "Can you help me with my oranges?"

Emily huffs, before turning off the engine. She still keeps her eye on Ezekiel Young and notices his figure approaching them. Monica senses Ezekiel's presence in her periphery and then chooses to react.

"Ezekiel Young, is this you now? My, how time flies!" Monica exclaims.

Emily looks at the man for any reaction but finds none.

"It sure does, Miss Monica." He tips his head to Emily's direction. "Miss Emily," he acknowledges.

He's still such a creep. Jesus, Monica! Emily thinks as

she watches him turns his attention back to Monica.

"So, what brings you over to Aliso Viejo? I thought you were in HQ?" Monica asks while pretending to rearrange her groceries. Ezekiel takes the hint and hands her the remaining oranges he scooped up.

"Some business," he says. Emily watches him shoot Monica with a menacing look. "There are vermin we need to clean out." An awkward beat. "From...my father's autobody shop."

"How nice!" Emily replies. "We're here on business too, though we'll fly back to SF tonight." She makes a show of getting out of the car with another grocery bag in hand and winds her arm around Monica's free one.

"Thanks for your help, Mr. Young." Emily stares pointedly at the man towering over her. "If you'll excuse us." Monica exchanges a look with Emily and follows her goodbye with a smile directed at the other man. "It was nice seeing you, Ezekiel."

The man bobs his head, lingers, but then returns to a car. The two women briskly walked to the entrance. Neither of them talks until they are safely inside the hotel lobby.

"That was fucking scary," Emily breaks the silence as soon as they sat themselves on a nearby couch. "And reckless. What the fuck was that about?"

"At least we know it's not much of a coincidence we saw two Fiducia members here," Monica says. She sighs with the weight of all the groceries in her hands. "Did you see how that man looked at me?"

Emily grimaces. "I was hoping you didn't see that."

"I'll be fine here, Em." Monica declares. "You need to get home for the pasiyam. I'll text you tonight for updates."

Emily pushes the elevator button for Monica. They nod in unison, not breaking eye contract until the door closes. She then creeps back outside. The coast is clear. She gets back in the car, fires it up, and heads directly home.

The night after the pasiyam is particularly restless. Emily recounts the Fiducia agents and assumes the paranoia was just all in her head. Even Bao, the ragdoll who likes warmth over everything else, sits on the windowsill and stares for most of the night. Even when she inches over to investigate what he is searching for, Bao does not react. Her weary eyes can't get past the shadows dancing under the streetlamps.

Emily chalks up the action as Bao being Bao. She closes her curtains a little more and hikes up her blanket higher before attempting to get some semblance of sleep. She tries and tries, checking her phone for Monica's delayed texts until the sun crests the horizon.

***

Emily hasn't had a good night's rest ever since Monica's hospitalization. That and ever since she got to Aliso Viejo, the paper cranes she meticulously folds in the daylight would unfurl like flowers that bloom in the night.

Most of the morning comes and goes with no update

from Monica. The encounters with two of Fiducia's top members spook Emily enough to stay home for the day, even if it means staying home with her mother and her brother. The three of them have not spoken about the argument, just existing around each other in silence. But Emily decides she can't ignore them forever. Keeping herself busy will be a good way to distract the gnawing anxiety and confusion that she is nursing.

The Wang household is quiet before the pasiyam, spare a few clangs that echo throughout the drab house. Since burying her father, the place has become tidier. There are only a few wayward medical paraphernalia. The bed is set to be sold on Craigslist. Most of the overflow of Chinese goods has been moved back to Xiào Lì until they figure out what to do with that situation.

Bao favors lounging in the downstairs living room now that that area has been cleaned the most. The ragdoll eagerly greets Emily as she enters the kitchen, and she is surprised that only Michael is there. He looks up and gives her a dismissive nod before going back to shredding chicken.

"Had breakfast?" Emily asks.

Michael hums. "Just tea."

"What are you making?"

"Some sandwiches for today's pasiyam," he answered.

That is where their conversations usually end in the short time that Emily is home. She would often cook for her brother, but she hasn't been able to ever since he went out of the country for college. They were close once, and Emily begins to miss it more now that she's back home. Rummaging through their refrigerator, she pulls out some eggs to make breakfast for the both of them.

"Mike?" Emily asks again.

"Hmm?"

"Are we okay?"

From the corner of her eyes, she sees her little brother cease the shredding. After a beat, he answers in a more somber tone. "We are."

"Not very convincing, dì di," Emily retorts.

"Shouldn't I be the one asking you that?" Michael's deep voice cuts in the symphony of sizzles from Emily's pan and the low whistle of the kettle Michael put on.

"I'm not sure if I've forgiven you for not telling me about Xiào Lì yet."

Michael nods at that. They move in sync in the kitchen, just like old times. While Emily plates the eggs and corned beef, her little brother expertly brews the oolong. Once done, Emily can't help the small smile that stretches on her face. It is an act that's been years removed. She and Michael head to their modest dining table. Michael clears off some bills and puts them aside for their plates.

"So, what are your plans now?" Emily casually asks after a sip of her tea. She is usually the first one to reach out to her little brother when they had a disagreement. Today is no different and their terse discussion folds into a crane line by line.

"Opening back up Xiào Lì, I guess," Michael mumbles with a mouthful of bread. "Can't have that go to waste now can we?"

"Is that what you really want?"

The siblings allow the silence to blanket over them like a second skin, each absorbed in their own meals. Emily fiddles with the scrambled eggs, and eyes her brother mimicking her.

"I can't leave Māma behind," Michael confesses.

"Mike, she's a grown woman," Emily huffs. "Of course you can."

Michael shakes his head. This wasn't the first time Emily had this conversation with her little brother. Between the two of them, Michael was always the more filial child. But this is the first time Emily has seen him so torn with his decision.

"Mike," Emily says yet again. "Didn't you say you wanted to intern in an immigrant law firm in Oakland? Did you talk about that with Māma? I'm sure she will understand."

"It's not that simple," he sighs. "Bàba's gone and we're in debt."

"We can work something out with the debt. I have ways. Especially now, let alone with Māma."

Michael gives her a tired stare. "Like, who will take care of Māma? She's old. She needs help around the house."

"I'm sure we can hire someone. You see all of the guests. Someone can check up on her or help. Volunteer around the store," she replies, exasperated. "C'mon, Mike. Do you really want to spend your life here?"

She watches her little brother's shoulder hunch a little as he returns his attention to his plate. He sips some tea and Emily can see him mull over some thoughts in his mind. Even when Michael is now older, he still hasn't shaken off his habit of playing with his food.

"I think I'll regret it if I leave," Michael speaks slowly. "I still haven't forgiven you either for not going home sooner." His admission shocks Emily before shame slithers in like a cold snake on her throat. Before she can let it consume her, Michael says something that completely catches her off guard.

"I know I will eventually," he whispers. "You're still my jiě jie."

They don't talk after that.

***

Monica's call arrives in the dead of the night. Relief and anger swirl in Emily's sleep-addled brain like a storm. She wants to give her a piece of her mind but in pure Monica fashion, she muscles her control over the conversation. She asks Emily to meet her early in the morning. Following the invitation, comes coordinates to a place right outside of town. Emily mulls the ideas over all night. The morning comes hard and fast, even with Bao's purring and slumber. She is meager in energy but gets out of bed anyway.

Emily's drive is unfamiliar and long. She is caught off-guard by the location. Unlike the highly curated Fiducia Instagram page, this place is far more subdued. It is a bland, hole-in-the-wall café close to sunny Aliso Viejo. Monica is different now. She is dressed in a drag sweatsuit. It makes her fit right in.

The pair heads to the table at the farthest corner of the shop after they pay for their orders. Monica gets a black Americano. An odd choice. Emily only sees her friend drink one after planning a charity event. Monica brings out a tablet from her bag and immediately loads up documents. Emily can't read from her side of the table. Once their drinks arrive, Monica begins chatting.

"Sorry if I've been radio silent."

"It's okay," Emily says to her friend. "If you tell me what's been going on with you and all this."

Monica purses her lips for a beat before exhaling. "Yeah...I needed time to process what I just learned."

Emily raises an eyebrow. "What do you mean?"

"Suzette called asking if we could video call. Sometime after you left me at the hotel."

"The financial adviser's wife? Aren't she and her husband big donors to Fiducia?" Emily huffs. "She's nuts if she thinks she's going to get answers from you."

"That's what I thought. But she said she wanted to show me something important."

"Well, did you believe her? It must have been a trap."

"I get what you mean, Em. But something in my gut told

me that I won't regret it if we hopped on a Zoom call."

Monica, ever the professional, does not once break eye contact with Emily. This is one of the tactics that Emily was first taught. Monica that she sees now is not the same mentor she had when they were discussing this technique. She has bags under her eyes and a haunted complexion that Emily has not seen on her before. Monica sips her coffee and begins explaining.

"I didn't want to leave the hotel until I got the full picture. I'm sorry for worrying you again.

She fiddles with her tablet. The device flashes a dull white color. Emily can't believe what she sees.

"These are..."

"They're Fiducia's financials of last fiscal year. When I called Casey out, she started to doubt Casey too." Monica leans over and zooms in on the title of the document. Large sums of numbers and a chart are below. "This was one of the first things she found when she was rummaging around her husband's files. I was already working with Ron to try and trace where my commissions were going, and this document matches with some of the exuberant charges in my name."

"Jet travel...suits...real estate? What the fuck was Casey doing?"

"Making himself rich off all of us."

Emily feels faint. The coffee doesn't heat organs. She recounts how some of their members come from financially unstable living conditions. She knows the affluent appearances they try to project. All this time she believed that this organization was built to help other people gain their confidence, to build their lives back together. That's what she's been telling her clients, who often confessed that they don't have much to give. It's because of Casey that their hard-earned money went to his luxuries. He was bleeding them all dry.

"How long has this been going on?" Emily whispers.

"Ron said he'll get back to me soon. Suzette thinks it's a little over 5 years running."

Immediate realization dawns on Emily like a freight train. "Wasn't the co-founder still around during that time?"

Monica gulps more coffee. "I believe so."

"Then what was she doing then? She didn't stop Casey?"

Monica grunts with a grimace. "That's what we're going to find out. We need to go back. Expose them right at the headquarters."

Emily recoils at that suggestion. "Mon, I know this is important to you. I'm nervous now, about all of this." Emily huffs. "My family is back home and struggling. I don't want to leave them just like that."

"This is something bigger than both of us, Em," Monica urges. "I don't want to allow him to steal from anyone else."

A large crash from the counter blows up their privacy. The women cover the tablet and look away. The other patrons hear it, too. A weary server drops a plate of food.

Monica still seemed perturbed.

"I think we've been here too long. Let's go back to the hotel." Monica says and makes a move to stand, but Emily reaches out her hand. Monica pauses and Emily's arm goes slack again.

"Yeah, let's talk about this back home."

"Your home." Monica spurts. A beat. "You sure your mom won't kick me out?"

"They were gone before I left. My Māma's doctor appointment. They may still be out. Besides, who knows if Ezekiel, or whoever weird shithead, is waiting for us at the hotel?"

Monica sighs. "Yeah. I have all I need here."

"How did you get here?" Emily says. Her coffee is fine to her now and grows antsy.

"Took Uber."

"Ok, I'll drive."

The pair stand and discard their cups in the trash. Monica pulls the door open for Emily. Bells clang onto the door. Monica steps out near the car and cheerfully says, "You drive I'll find a playlist."

The drive back to the suburbs turns into karaoke. They sing and dance in their seats as their world becomes increasingly unrecognizable. It makes the women lively and control of the moment. Emily turns down more familiar, scenic roads. Coasting the car now, she shuts her eyes for a moment, hoping that this part of her life would end so she could move on. When she opens, the car is close to Emily's home. She spots the old Ford pickup truck parked in the driveway.

"Shit, Michael's back."

"And that's a problem?" Monica asks.

"He's going through stuff and we're patching up things—"

"He seems nice. He visited you at Fiducia, right?"

Emily sighs and parks on the street.

"Maybe we can help him with that. Isn't that what we are good at?"

Monica declares this with a smile and gets out of the car striding to the front door. Emily sighs and beckons Monica to the rear. As soon as Emily opens the door, the pair is greeted with a busy kitchen. The smell of pork wafts in the air. Various spices are on the counter without their caps on. Michael is in the center of the chaos, meticulously arranging freshly made wrappers.

"Hey," Emily says nonchalantly.

"Hey," Michael responds, rolling out another piece of dough. When he looks up he spots Monica coming inside the busy kitchen.

Emily speaks louder this time. "This is Monica. I think you remember her from before."

"Hi Michael!" Monica shouts. She steps forward and goes in for a confident handshake. "It's nice to meet you, formally."

Michael shoots her a warm smile. He wipes his hands on his apron before shaking her hand. They linger for a moment and let go. "It's nice to meet you, Monica. Sorry for the mess."

"Nonsense. A busy kitchen is my home."

Emily blanches. She knows Monica can't cook anything to save her life. Monica gives Emily a nudge with her elbow.

"Emily is a testament to how good I am. Right, Em?"

"Right," she snorts and ushers Monica to the living room. "We'll just be in there to talk. Shout if you need anything, Michael."

Michael waves a dismissive hand and continues the food preparation. Monica catches this as an opportunity.

"We'll help you!"

Emily elbows her friend back. They exchange a glance, almost like telepathy. But Monica heads back to the counter. She looks so lively now. A look Emily remembers before. Her mentor and friend now back to her roots. Emily joins the pair and Michael sorts some bowls for the women. He isn't pouting, which is already a win for Emily.

"Em folds the cleanest dumplings in this house. She can teach you." The comment surprises Emily further. Wasn't he upset at her? "Isn't that right, Em?" Guess not.

Emily snorts again. She eyes up a few wrappers and the muscle memory reacquaint her fingers.

"Sounds great," Monica exclaims. She inspects a spatula and picks it up. "Where do we begin?"

Michael is quick to delegate the tasks. Monica and Emily dutifully fold wontons and set them aside, while Michael tends to the filling cooking on the stove. Emily is diligent in teaching Monica how to wrap and fold, but she really doesn't have a hard time. With the third wonton, Monica can get the hang of putting the right amount of filling to properly fold the wonton. By the seventh, she is creating little pleats without Emily's instructions.

"So, how many are we doing?" Monica asks. She is calm while making the food now. Similar to the meetings, it provides tranquility for the group.

"About 60," Michael answers.

"60? How many people are you feeding?"

Emily hums. She finishes her tenth wonton and is inspecting the finished ones before arranging them in a row. "There's been 20 or so people going to our pasiyam. Might be more today."

"We usually prepare extras for people to take home," Michael adds. "People love Māma's dumplings, so this is usually the first dish to go during parties."

"Oh! So, you cook a lot?" Monica says with glee.

"Yeah, and I'm good at it too." Micheal responds over the sizzle of his old wok.

The smell of star anise and five spice wafts in the air as Michael expertly sautés the pork with the other aromatics. Emily ferries an empty tray from the counter to the table, she can't help but smile at her brother's pleased expression. Bao joins them briefly, butting his head to the legs of the family and sniffing the guest. Michael continues the discussion.

"Māma asked Em a lot to help since she and Bàba

worked till late. I got interested as a kid. I started to cook on my own in middle school."

"Impressive, Michael," Monica says.

Michael smiles as deposits freshly cooked filling on an adjacent tray. He swiftly folds three more wontons to fill up the tray. The hint of cinnamon becomes more prominent once the dish is closer to them. It is a feat for Emily to not grab a spoonful like she always did when her mother was making this. Luckily, her brother had the same idea and gave her and Monica a teaspoon to taste.

"Oh, my goodness, Michael. This is so delicious. You should totally turn this into a business!"

Michael shoots her a bashful smile. His cheeks blush. "Thanks, maybe I should."

"He cooks as good as Māma," Emily adds. "We really didn't have much takeout because we couldn't afford it. But I really didn't care for it at that time because I could just ask Micheal to cook for me sometimes."

"Where's Mrs. Wang by the way?" Monica inquires.

Michael doesn't miss a beat. "She's out spending time with some locals. We ran out of hoisin sauce today, too. She can't make her special sauce without it."

Monica giggles. "Special sauce?"

Emily nods, a giggle also escaping her lips. "She can be very anal about her recipes. If it's not done the right way, she has a fit for days."

"Yeah, but she especially gets fussy with her wontons though," Michael continues. "But they're the best when we make them for celebrations. Pasiyams are celebrations in my opinion," Michael washes his hands. "We pray because we want Bàba's soul to be safe when he departs from this world."

"I think Māma is also doing this out of guilt, Mike," Emily interjects. Michael furrows his brows but says nothing. Emily continues. "She doesn't exactly pray quietly."

Michael snorts. "True."

"Maybe she missed your Bàba a little extra that day," Monica comments.

"Maybe we all miss him a little extra," Emily adds. "I still don't like doing it. Loud prayers."

Michael huffs. "It's what Māma wants to do. I'm not a fan of the loud praying either, for the record."

Emily stays quiet for a moment, debating whether she voices out her grievances. She does. "Then why not tell her you don't like it? Why does it seem like you're a pushover for Māma?"

Michael freezes. Some of the filling he was holding spills on the plate. Michael takes it personally, and gazes at Emily with contrition.

"Life wasn't easy when you last left, jiě jie."

Emily continues to stare at her younger brother, not knowing what to say. Is she supposed to apologize? Is she supposed to throw a tantrum? To her, it feels as though she is speaking to someone so far away from her. The sinking feeling of shame and grief pools in her stomach, and it coats the pristine paper cranes. She is aware that things have changed without her, but she still couldn't accept that she has. Not without the guilt of leaving. Not without the burden of being their eldest daughter who ran off and avoided responsibility.

"Michael, I want you to be—"

Suddenly, a clatter from the back door surprises everyone. Michael breaks off eye contact and steps over to investigate. "Bao must have gotten out," Michael says and heads towards the screen door. Emily expects to hear the poor cat's howling, but instead it's her brother humming in confusion. "I'm sorry, can I help you?"

Monica is the first to react. She notes a figure looking into the home. "Is that really her? Cheri?"

Emily is not having it. She stomps over to the door, shoving Michael away. The half-folded wonton flies out of her hand. Bao is in fact still in the house. He sees the wonton and mews before dragging it into the dining area. Emily greets the woman with a stern, furrowed brow. Similar to her absent mother.

"What are you doing here on my property?"

Instead of Cheri's usually fashionable attire, she shows up with a ratty shirt and some denim pants that Emily has never seen her wear outside the office. Her usually well-kept hairdo is scrunched up in a messy bun, which exposes her fraying hair extensions. Cheri's usually confident demeanor is gone and what faces Emily is a shell of one of Fiducia's elite.

"I'm here to take you both back, you traitors!"

"Traitors?" Monica raises her eyebrow. "Where the hell did you get that?"

"Casey has been running around the place trying to cover up whatever shit you left in the open, Monica," Cheri says in between gritted teeth. "We all trusted you, and this is how you repay us?"

Emily sees Monica seethe from where she was standing, and she immediately attempts to calm her down. As soon as she places her hands on her mentor's arm, she shrugs her off and marches toward Cheri. When Cheri sees the fire in Monica's eyes she wasn't able to stop herself from stepping back.

"What I have done for Fiducia is all thankless efforts! How dare you say that to me?"

"Mon, come on," Emily says, trying to hold her friend back. "Mon, it's not worth it."

"Effort? What effort? You just went out and paraded your sob story so you could sell a course. You're the reason why Fiducia is in trouble right now!" Cheri shouts back.

Michael inserts himself between the women and puts his arm out. "This, whatever it is, needs to stop!"

"How dare you!" Monica screams. She dips below Michael and lunges at Cheri. Emily winds her arms tightly around Monica's midsection before contact is made.

"Fiducia is in trouble because Casey is a corrupt asshole, Cheri!" Monica says, panting and squirming. "Open your eyes!"

Cheri clenches her teeth before stepping forward to claw at Monica. Cheri lashes out to dig her nails into Monica's face. Michael takes the brunt of the intruder's attack. He grunts as her fingers dig into his chest. Emily is thankful he didn't stop going to the gym.

"Casey is doing everything in his power to fix everything you broke, you bitch!" Cheri yells as she still tries to break free from Michael's grip.

"You think just because you're fucking Casey that makes you safe? He's never going to marry you!" Monica continues to shout. "He is using you, me, and everyone else."

"Casey loves me!"

"Oh yeah?" Monica challenges. She lunges at Cheri as well but is forced back by Emily's attempts to contain her. Emily feels her grip weaken from Monica's incessant struggle. Every word Monica speaks is punctuated by an aural stab. "Casey's in Seattle.. with Gina."

Cheri pinches her lips. "What the fuck does have got to do with anything?"

Cheri morphs into a conflicted expression. A switch has been flipped in her mind, and her body sagged in Michael's arms.

"You get it now?" Monica simmers down. "Casey takes you on business trips like that. Why didn't he take you this time?"

"I...he said he needed Gina there," Cheri barely manages to stutter out. "Casey said he loves me! You're lying!"

"For fuck's sake, Cheri! He already replaced you!"

The sound of a car door shutting and a familiar voice echo from the front. Mrs. Wang enters the home with two bags of groceries. Emily lets go of Monica and tries to distract her mother, yet to no avail. Mrs. Wang blankly stares at the group of calming, tired humans.

"I leave for a few hours, and this is what I get." Mrs. Wang says before turning to a now crying Cheri "Who is she and why are you crying in my house?"

Emily murmurs to Michael to get Cheri out of there. He obliges and ushers the sobbing woman away and down the block. Monica inhales and buttons her clothes that are ruffled in the scuffle.

"Good afternoon, Mrs. Wang," Monica says with calm composure. "Nothing more to see here."

"I see you've brought more trouble to my doorstep," Mrs. Wang chides. The frost in her voice doubles the heaviness of the atmosphere. Emily and Monica have dealt with difficult clients in the past, but this was the first time Monica was too stunned to speak.

"Māma," Emily interjects. "It was the other woman who tried to bother us. Monica's been helping Mike and I prepare for the pasiyam."

"This has been the second time *she* comes here, and a fight erupts," Mrs. Wang says, not taking her eyes off Monica. Michael returns inside and speaks brief Mandarin to his mother. But all he sees is her downturned lips and sad eyes. Monica reflects this as a tactic, something she only does when comforting clients dealing with grief.

"I'm sorry if you feel that way, Mrs. Wang," Monica starts. "But do not worry. I will not stay long." She turns to her friend with an apologetic smile. "Em, I'll take Cheri out for a late lunch. Meet us there when you can?"

Emily feels a jolt and tries to mumble a response, but Monica's stare leaves no room for argument. There are no words exchanged between them after that. Monica excuses herself from the room with poise with neither of the Wangs acknowledging her fleeting presence. Mrs. Wang quietly complains about the mess and lugs the groceries on the counter. Michael returns inside, wiping his shirt.

"They took Cheri's car, jiě jie," Michael says. "That was intense."

Emily nods. "Monica can handle herself I think."

Michael nods and starts to clean up the kitchen while Emily tries to sort out the groceries. Mrs. Wang scuffles around the kitchen, gathering the ingredients she uses for the special sauce. She inspects the finished wontons and addresses Emily.

"Lì, did I not tell you that stranger is not welcome here?" Mrs. Wang berates her, not looking at her and instead focusing on making her sauce. "She's disrupted your father's ceremony and brings more disrespectful people here."

"She's not a stranger, Māma," Emily says in defense "Her name is Monica. She's my friend from San Francisco.

I told you this last time. You can't be rude to a guest that I brought home."

"I can and I will because this is my house, Lì. I have the right."

"Māma, I told you it wasn't her fault. It was Cheri who started screaming!"

"Enough, the both of you!" Michael shouts. He wants to pull Emily away for a private accosting, but Emily pins him down with a stare.

"No Mike, stay out of this. I'm sick and tired of just holding what I want to say!" Palpable exasperation lingers in her voice. "Māma, you're not the only one who lost Bàba. If I decide my friends can grieve with me, I can."

A wooden spoon slams on their countertop. It snaps and pieces clatter on the floor. The bowl of soy sauce is flies from Mrs. Wang's hands and into the sink. Emily tracks the bowl and feels a splash of soy on her arms. She is shocked by her mother's sudden gush of vitriol.

"I have been very patient with you for years, Lì," Mrs. Wang says. "But that selfishness has got to stop. If you're living here then this insolence has got to stop." Mrs. Wang emphasizes every word, and that lights a bigger fire in Emily.

"Selfish? You're the one who asked me to live here, Māma! I'm not the selfish one here. You are!"

"Stop it, jiě jie!" This time, Michael grabs Mrs. Wang's shoulders to pull her back. He curses in Mandarin that flies above Emily's head and falls on her mother's deaf ears. Mrs.

Wang points the splintered spoon at Emily. It is the most threatening the woman has ever looked.

"You spent all this time in San Francisco and left us here," Mrs. Wang's yelling continues. "To go broke, to die, even. That's you being selfish!"

"Fine, you want to know the truth? I didn't go home because I didn't want to see you," Emily seethes in place. "That was all because I couldn't stand your micromanaging and controlling every inch of my life."

An afternoon breeze chills the kitchen. Mrs. Wang's brow hardens with thick creases. "How dare you say that to me." Venom drips from her words.

Michael gently nudges his mother, but she is concrete and unbudging. "Stop, jiě jie. We can all talk about this calmly later. The guests are coming, and food needs to be plated. Come on, Māma, you should get changed."

Mrs. Wang drops the splintered spoon and stares out to nothing in particular as if in a trance. "I was the one who sacrificed everything to give us a better life. Bless your father, but the burden was mine and mine alone. I was the one who fought with immigration so you both could thrive in the USA. The one thing I ask, you cannot even do. I just asked you to respect my wishes to not bring this woman here. Is that so difficult to understand?"

Emily feels her hackles rise as high as her voice. All the instinct of respecting her mother that was drilled into her since she was a child shriveled up in the fire of her anger.

"Just because you were never loved doesn't mean you

can take it out on me! It's not my fault your life was hard!"

"Emily, that's enough!" Michael shouts, which makes their mother jump slightly. "This is insane!"

"What, Mike? You feel the same way! You've been under Ma's control for years! She only wants me here to pay for her bills and she wants you here to take care of her."

The kitchen boils its occupants like a pressure cooker and an uncomfortable silence envelops. Emily sees her mother grip her brother's shirt, but this does not deter her from challenging her mother's vitriol. Not when her mother is openly hostile. Michael tries to coax her again to leave, nearly stepping out completely. Emily is impressed that her little brother tries to get their mother out of their room, but she knows where she got her stubbornness from, and it wasn't from her father. Mrs. Wang uses the lull to continue her tirade.

"We sacrificed everything to make ends meet for your Bàba. We even asked Michael to come home because we didn't want to bother you in San Francisco. You were supposed to help me keep this family together. Yet every time I turn to you, you become the reason this family is in crisis. Because you're selfish. You're so full of yourself, you don't even understand how easy you had it!"

"Easy?" Emily finds herself laughing at the disbelief she feels at her mother's words. "Being the daughter of the most selfish mother is the hardest life anyone could have. Do not take out your anger on me because I have the freedom you never had."

Mrs. Wang goes limp in Michael's arms. Never in Emily's life has she seen her mother look this devastated. But the surprise is yet to come. With deft movements, Mrs. Wang maneuvers out of her son's protective arms. She stomps over and slaps Emily clean on the cheek. Emily does not register the pain, even though a loud thwack echoes in the room. Michael's deescalating shout is the only thing that shakes Emily up from her stupor.

"I..." Emily pushes out of her throat. Burning flesh makes her eye twitch. "I'm sorry."

The sharp inhale of her mother signals to Emily that she was successful in what she sought to do. A hollow victory. Mrs. Wang ignores her apology. Michael is struck by distress as he escorts their mother away. Emily feels the tears prickle her eyes. The irreversible damage has been done.

"I'm...I'm going out. Taking the truck," Emily whispers to no one.

She heads out of the house as fast as she can. Guests arrive as she drives off.

***

The harsh overhead lights of Panera do nothing to hide the bruise around Emily's eye, nor the ghastly complexion of embarrassment and shame. One concerned look from Monica tells Emily that she looks like absolute shit. The pain pools through her ankles. She can't swallow her food, let alone the dreading guilt asphyxiating her lungs. She tries—countless times—to make scenes of the argument into delicate paper cranes but they singe into a fireball with to her touch.

"Got you an agave lemonade when you texted, but I think you need a stronger drink," Monica says, assuredly, and hands her the drink. "Gonna eat those chips?"

Emily gratefully takes a sip of the drink offered to her.

"Want to tell me what happened to your cheek?" Monica asks.

Emily shakes her head. "Not right now. I think I need to sit with this." She sips and then looks at Monica's side of the table. "You didn't get food?"

Monica shakes her head.

Emily holds the cold drink to her face and scans the restaurant. "Where's Cheri?"

"Cheri went back to her hotel as soon as we were done talking. I think she also had some things to sort out." Monica downs the last of her latte. "I convinced her to testify."

"That's huge. I'm glad you could persuade her to go against Casey."

Monica flashes her teeth. A true, Monica smile. "I think she knows the truth now."

"I bet she still fought tooth and nail all the way to Panera."

Soft giggles ring between the pair. "Oh, hell yes. I'm surprised she didn't, like, stab me with the car keys. Casey betraying her is the worst kind of sin. She's so hellbent on getting her revenge." Monica pauses, hunches closer. "We're taking notes today and leaving tomorrow."

Emily's eyes widen. She flinches from her developing bruise. "What?"

"Listen, Em. I don't want to do this without you," Monica says while leveling her with a look. "But Cheri says Casey's been planning something big since before Washington. That means we have to move quicker before he catches wind of what we're trying to do."

But can we trust her? Emily thinks to herself.

"I'd ask you to come with us, but I know you have your own things to sort out here," Monica assures. "You can help once the pasiyam is done."

After a beat, Emily whispers. "Do I not get the choice in this?"

"What do you mean?" Monica asks, bewilderment coloring her words.

"You decided that I can't come because of my family." Anger pushes the words out of Emily's mouth. "Do I not get a choice in this?"

"You told me your decision this morning."

Emily huffs. "Well, I'm fucking changing it."

Monica purses her lips into a thin line. "You don't have to push yourself, Em. This will be an uphill battle until he's locked up."

"And I'm not pushing myself." The tears pricking her eyes make their way down her cheeks. She wipes them off with one hand and sighs. "I want to go, Monica."

"Are you sure? And this is not because of what happened?"

Emily bristles but shakes her head. "This is something I'm doing for myself."

***

Monica books early morning tickets for San Francisco. The pair hug and Emily goes back home. After the pasiyam, she must face her brother and mother once again. Though Mrs. Wang has not once emerged from her room, Emily and Michael settle amicably, but not without a tearful apology.

Emily is surprised she gets any sleep at all. Even more so, she is surprised at herself that her resolve has not wavered overnight. This decision is far away from the peace she has been yearning for since Becca's passing. She feels strangely at peace with it. In the peeking light of dawn, the first thing she sees is her dark gray ceiling. She pulls away from the warmth of her wrong pillows, folds her wrong blanket neatly like how her mother taught her, and finally opens the creaky window. Her father is still dead. Becca is still dead. Fiducia is still up and running. Emily is determined to change the only being she can.

Bao scratches at her door, forcing her to get up from her bed like clockwork. The ragdoll cat sashays to her bed like he owns the place and jumps into her open suitcase on the floor. Emily picks Bao up enough times until he gets the idea. She packs her If she stays in Aliso Viejo, the less of an impact she can make when it comes to Fiducia's ultimate downfall. Besides, she is tired of feeling like a small soul trying to drag the dead weight of a body through life. She wants to do something tangible, something good to make up for all the problems she's caused.

At first, Emily wants to leave without saying goodbye, but something in that idea does not sit well with her. Rustling in the other bedrooms makes Emily jump to action. Dressed and ready, she picks up Bao from his resting spot and carries him like a baby in one hand and the suitcase in the other. Steeling her resolve, she takes a deep breath before stepping out of her room only to meet her little brother going out of his own room.

"Em, are you really going?" Michael asks curiously, assessing her.

Emily expects some kind of negative reaction from her brother, but this is much different. The warmth that envelops her catches both of them off guard. Bao wriggles from her arm and lands on the banister. The pair stands like that for a few beats. Michael easily towers over his sister. He could just prevent her from leaving. Instead, errant sniffles come from him. Emily, with tears staining hasty mascara, hugs him with one arm.

"You were always the worst crybaby between us," Emily says as a joke.

"And you're still my jiě jie," Michael replies, tightening his arms around Emily.

They stay still for a few more moments. Emily is conflicted because she isn't sure when she is going to see her little brother again. She knows Monica's directives are risky, possibly criminal. Emily refuses to drag both of them towards the inevitable warpath Casey is on.

"You take care," Michael says, pulling away from the hug. "Take them down and come back for dumpling night, all right?" Emily nods before going downstairs to the kitchen, lugging her suitcase behind her. She crushes the heavy disappointment when she doesn't find her mother in her usual spot. Where she'd nurse a warm cup of oolong tea. She regrets those dagger-like words she used on her mother yesterday and doesn't blame her for not saying goodbye.

Atop the vacant table in the kitchen lies a steaming cup of tea. The hot air wafts through the dancing beams of the sun and Emily cautiously approaches it. Once near enough, she finds a small letter with the neatest handwriting she has ever seen. Scribbled on top is her full name in Mandarin. Her eyes flit from the letter and the cup, and she begins to sob.

Smelling the fragrance, Emily slowly drinks the tea. Tranquility washes over, albeit briefly, while she is doing nothing but drinking. The message her mother leaves her is true and memorable, something she can take with her anywhere. In no time, the tea is gone and her cup rests gently in the sink. She folds the letter into a two-dimensional paper crane, before tucking it into her pocket.

Emily walks her body and suitcase to the front door.

Their old family photo stares back. In it, everyone looks so happy, standing with hands on shoulders and teeth bare. Briefly, she wonders if they will ever be that happy again, but something in Emily thinks that they will, sometime, some years later. She opens the door, and bids goodbye to Bao. One last pet met with one last purr. He wraps his tail around her, and she leaves.

About The Author

David Estringel is a Xicanx writer & poet with works published in literary magazines and journals, such as, *The Opiate, Azahares, Cephalo Press, Sledgehammer Lit, Ethel, Literary Heist, Cowboy Jamboree, San Antonio Review, Punk Noir Magazine, Poetry NI, Dreich, Somos en escrito, Fahmidan Journal, Ethel, The Milk House, Beir Bua Journal*, and *Roi Faineant*. He is the author of multiple books, including *Indelible Fingerprints* (Alien Buddha Press, 2019), *Cold Comfort House*, (Anxiety Press, 2022), *Blind Turns in the Kitchen Sink* (Anxiety Press, 2023), the chapbooks, *PeripherieS* (The Bitchin' Kitsch, 2020), *Eating Pears on the Rooftop* (Finishing Line Press, 2022), and more. David is a collegiate professor, editor-in-chief at *The Argyle Literary Magazine*, and poetry editor at *The Temz Review*. Connect with David on X: @The_Booky_Man and his website: www.davidestringel.com

About The Author

Alexandra Naughton is a writer based in Philadelphia, Pennsylvania. She is the founder and editor-in-chief of Be About It Press, established in 2010. She is the author of several poetry collections including *a place a feeling something he said to you* (Spooky Girlfriend Press, 2020), *You Could Never Objectify Me More Than I've Already Objectified Myself* (Punk Hostage Press, 2015), *I Will Always Be In Love* (Paper Press, 2015), and *I Wish You Never Emailed Me* (Ghost City Press, 2016). Her first novel, *American Mary* (Civil Coping Mechanisms, 2016) is republished as a serial on her Substack, *talk about it*. Her writing has been widely published on the web and in print, and she co-hosts the reading series, "Bring A Blanket" in Philadelphia. Find her on Instagram, X, Facebook, and Patreon.

About The Author

Risha Mae Ordas is a writer, poet, and psychology professor. Her works have appeared or are forthcoming in *Novice*, *Moonbow Magazine*, *Afterpast Review*, and *Porchlit Magazine*. She is based in Baguio City, Philippines. *Escaping Emily* is her long-form fiction debut.

About the Publisher

Follow us on:

Scan the QR code to visit us

www.thirtywestph.com